Contents

Skarda   *1*

In the Secret Places of the Stairs   *21*

An American Presence   *41*

The Ghost of Sandburg's Phizzog   *63*

Dwelling   *83*

The Chair Trick   *101*

This Horse of a Body of Mine   *117*

The Landscaper   *139*

Stars   *163*

for Harry Mark Petrakis
and the writer's age-old myths

... the writer is searching for something. I have no idea what, and neither does he. How meaningless, how insane the searching of others is. And what of our own? Does he see me as I see him, lost, anxious, alone? Capturing life in a book, taking time's measurements. That's writing. Giving conventional dimensions to existence. One manipulates time for artistic effect, thus ruling, falsely, secretly, over one's own life.

The writer dreams of a book, a woman, a distant city.

There is another sort of writer — I for one — who stretches one book over an entire lifetime. When I finish one book, I begin another immediately. One cannot allow the blood of time to drain away drop by drop.

A woman, a book, a city. The writer's age-old myths.

The writer's blood is time.

We go through life in flames, and nobody warns us that we are on fire so as not to frighten us. We slowly make our way through the city amid patches of light and darkness, heading nowhere, talking, dreaming, braving the cold, fear, shadows, driving past vast holes of time, streets fast asleep, multitudes.

— Francisco Umbral
A Mortal Spring

Skarda

I was left with Babi in the basement. The blood of freshly killed chickens in the coal bin; the secrets of Grandpa's locks and keys; and the visits of Skarda, her burlap bag of chickens, and her cloth coat trimmed in fox with beautiful glass eyes that I touched and rubbed. Skarda, the card lady, who saw I would be left with all this.

Babi lived in a long brick bungalow on Pulaski Road in Chicago. The front entrance to the house was never used. The first floor contained a parlor, a dining room, two bedrooms, and a kitchen, all of it untouched, uninhabited except when Babi went up there to dust, and I sometimes followed her. There was red crystal from Prague in glass cases. There were Oriental rugs on the floor that I would trace, in patterns, over and over again till my fingers burned, till I became rivers and trees and birds. The sofa and chairs were decorated with Babi's intricate white crocheted doilies — stars, they appeared to me, or snowflakes, tied endlessly together. In the dining room, a crocheted tablecloth covered the entire length and width of the table and fell halfway down to the floor. Hiding beneath there as a child, I looked out on flowered wallpaper, a darkened doorway, Babi, windows and light all in pieces yet held together in Babi's handiwork.

The kitchen floor was covered in gray linoleum with small bands of red, yellow, green, and blue. Polished frequently and smelling of wax, the surface, touched by sunlight, possessed a density, a glow not unlike ice. There was a cream enameled gas stove against the wall and a small white refrigerator that stood empty. Empty as the entire house, on this floor, stood empty. Empty as a museum, as a show-

case, as a setting where people who came to this country with nothing began to accumulate things that spoke of Old World royalty, New World possessions, and were uncertain how to live with all this, except with reverence and a sense of keeping things unspoiled.

In the corner of the kitchen was a highly varnished door with a silver key that led beyond to an attic where I slept one winter night, under a *pesina*, a feather comforter that Babi had made of down and carried with her aboard ship when she crossed from the Old Country to meet my grandfather, who had come to New York from Hungary a year before her.

It was in the basement where Babi lived, where she cooked, where visitors and relatives gathered, where Grandpa came at night after work at the icehouse, and where smells of soup, herbs, spices, chicken, rabbit, sweet-sour sauces, and fresh bakery always lingered.

The world opened slowly to my eyes. I claimed nothing but images of no design. Strange tongues in the basement. Words barely understood. The screech and blue flash of streetcars curving out of the neighborhood. The pattern of red brick streets with moss growing in-between. Gypsies in storefront windows. The smell of stale beer behind corner tavern doors. The silver Zephyr that sped by on the tracks a few doors down from Babi's. Uncle Frankie, who had gone away and left his set of drums with the colored lights inside in the basement. Uncle Tim, who sold fruit and vegetables in the market and drank alone on the bench in Babi's backyard every Sunday afternoon. The second-floor flat with the black fire escape where I lived with my mother and

SKARDA

father some distance from Babi. And the summer night I walked home with my father from Babi's, my head back, dizzily watching the sky filled with stars and a full moon. We passed a fence, and I bagan climbing it, wanting to be closer to all I could see up there. Hoping to touch it.

You can't do that, said my father. You can't ever get close to it.

On her way to work each morning, my mother took me around the back of Babi's house and down the gangway filled with the smell of roasted coffee from the warehouse next door. Bunches of red and white peonies grew along the side of the house in summer, mixing their scent with the coffee smells next door and the fragrance of the flowers in Babi's backyard. The silver metal gate clicked open and shut as we moved down the concrete steps to the basement kitchen, where Babi fed a fire in the black stove and busied her hands with wooden spoons.

She spoke to her daughter, my mother, in Czech. There was often anger in Babi's face. As a child I cowered before the uncertainties of her mood from moment to moment. She might ignore my mother for minutes, then both their voices would rise, fall to a whisper, then rise again. Silence. Babi would push aside pots, drop spoons on the table, wipe her hands in her apron, and suddenly engulf me with her huge body, holding my neck in the crook of her arm, tight against her aproned breast.

As she slowly released me, kissing the top of my head, clucking sounds in a foreign tongue, I would stand beside her, my face smudged in baking flour, watching her pull tiny pieces of dough stuck to her

fingers, fiercely hurling language again at my mother, turning her back to her, opening and closing the oven, picking up the wooden spoons once more to stir and settle the pots vibrating on the stove.

Without speaking, Mother would kiss me goodbye and leave me alone with Babi, who would continue to talk to herself while she cooked, sometimes curse and cry, sometimes hum and sing. Throughout the day she would both forget and remember that I was there, giving me soup to taste in a spoon, finding a pencil and paper for me to draw at the table, taking out a glass of old, discolored dice in a cabinet to play bunco or a worn deck of blue pinochle cards, speaking to me—hands, arms, face, mouth—in a language I slowly began to absorb but could not voice.

We sat across from each other at the table while she took the bunco dice in the glass, talking to them, talking to me, pointing to the number three, her favorite, counting the threes as they tumbled from the glass onto the oilcloth. She was happy when her numbers came, her points accumulated. She cursed when things were against her. I feared the sounds that came out of her then; how she transferred her ill fortune to everything around her, including me.

I wanted the game over with; I wanted her to win. I wanted to be out of her sight. I slipped under the table when she brought the bottom of the glass down hard in frustration, quitting, spilling the dice onto the floor, thrusting her chair into the wall, returning to the stove in a heavy, sidestep motion, rocking on her feet. I inched my way out to the backyard to watch the goldfish in the pond and feed them crumbs I had pocketed from the kitchen table.

SKARDA

I stretched out on my stomach and watched them swim into my face. I called to them, imitating the sounds I had heard Babi make, luring them to her hands. They were the same color as the fire she fed in the stove, the flames behind the furnace door in winter.

Often when I looked up, Babi would be on her knees in a nearby flower bed, murmuring, digging around the plants with a large metal spoon. On her head was Grandpa's old straw hat to shield her face from the sun. She paid no mind to me.

I would drift down to the basement when I was hungry, and she would sense this. She would pick up a round loaf of homemade rye and, with a butcher knife that hung beneath the table, hold the bread tight against her breast and begin slicing it unevenly toward her heart. She would take soupbones from a pot on the stove, blow the steaming marrow onto the slice of rye bread, sprinkle it with salt, take a bite of it herself, and give me the rest. Then she would wash the bones clean and set them before me as playthings. Not a word would be said.

The front of the basement, where I sometimes ventured to get out of Babi's way, was always cooler, except in winter when the furnace burned and firelight from the slots on the furnace door danced on the cement floor.

There were clean white curtains on all the windows, with the shades halfway drawn. A few wooden chairs stood against the whitewashed walls and Uncle Frankie's set of drums in a far corner up front. Locks hung from all the cabinets and from Grandpa's wooden tool chests.

THE GHOST OF SANDBURG'S PHIZZOG

He was a man of locks and keys. A man who was always missing things and always accusing others of stealing from him—his own children, Skarda, even Babi herself. Someone, he was certain, was breaking into his garage at night, stealing wood, garden tools, whatever he could not find. Someone was taking tools from him. Someone was stealing money from the cabinets in the basement. The icehouse was full of thieves.

A heavy brass lock hung from the garage door. Silver locks glinted all around the basement. Every door in the house had a key in it and the lock was turned; the key in the door for the basement to the upstairs was tied to the doorknob with string.

Grandpa, I could understand. He spoke English and joked with me. Skarda, the card lady, is coming, he sometimes teased me. Skarda will steal you, he laughed, and I would run away and hide. There was no mystery to him except for the locks, a golden earring of Babi's that came from his Gypsy past, and the sudden anger he would pour upon her as he reverted to his native tongue, the two of them lost to me in terror while I awaited rescue in a language I could comprehend.

We lived a distance from Babi that I measured in steel tracks: the blue flash of the sparking streetcars heading into the city; the silver streak of the Zephyr slicing the darkness with a moan. We lived high in a second-floor flat above a drugstore with cardboard figures of women in the front window, advertising Colgate toothpaste and Kodak film. The stairway always smelled of iodine. A black iron fire escape hung from the side of the building, outside my

SKARDA

bedroom window, like the folded wing of a dark bird. Though my father explained the mechanism to me, I was never certain how it worked since only in a fire would the desperate weight of us—possible victims seeking salvation—offset the balance and set us free.

In the upstairs flat the three of us took our meals, spoke only English, and remained quietly somewhat above it all. We sat at a shiny enamel table with chrome legs. My mother cooked American for my father's sake. The smell of boiling coffee is all I remember. The old wallpaper had been steamed and scraped off in the living room and the walls painted a color called baby blue. A solid gray carpet of no pattern covered the floor. The sofa was protected with a throw-over muslin sheet. Pinned to the back of an old maroon armchair was a large crocheted doily Babi had made in the shape of a star. After supper we listened to the radio in the living room. I stared out the window at the people on the street below, waited for the streetlights to go on, and then went to bed.

On Saturday mornings the three of us walked to 26th Street to shop for meat and groceries. There were barrels of live carp in front of the butcher shop. I would put my hand in, feel the cool water rise to my elbow, and try to touch them. In the fall, dead rabbits hung from the awning above the butcher's window, and I would touch their fur and be reminded of the fox on Skarda's coat. On Sunday afternoon we went down to the drugstore, where I was treated to a Big Top chocolate ice-cream cone, the ice cream itself packaged, cone shaped, in thin cardboard which the druggist carefully removed before tucking the ice cream firmly into the sugar cone. Sometimes we

would walk to Babi's and sit in the backyard for a short while. On Sunday evening there was Jack Benny on the radio; there were men carrying home buckets of beer on the street below; there were the streetlights coming on, and then bed and the shadow of the fire escape, the shadow of the ring of the shade-pull fixing a small, luminous moon on my wall for the night. On Monday morning I would be left with Babi.

One afternoon in winter Skarda appeared in the basement without warning, handing Babi a sack of chickens, which she carried to the coal bin. Skarda put her black leather shopping bag on a chair and hung her fox-trimmed coat over mine on the coatrack that stood near the doorway to the front of the basement. In summer I would rush into the backyard out of her sight. In winter I was trapped inside. I hid in the front basement behind the drums, refusing her handfuls of hard candy, her calls to come out and see her. After she and Babi had talked awhile, I sneaked into the kitchen, behind the coatrack, the fox rubbing against my face.

They sat across from each other at the table, drinking coffee, eating fresh bakery that Babi had made earlier in the morning. They spoke in a different language, Hungarian, and their hands flew. Skarda was thinner, darker, younger than Babi. Small curls of black hair seemed squeezed from beneath a purple cap that she never removed from her head. She wore, always, a black shawl over a paisley garment that hung down to her feet. There was a quickness about her, a richness so different from Babi, who seemed so heavy and tired, so thick in her arms, so despairing in

SKARDA

her apron of flour and blood, grease and handprints. The fingers of Skarda's hands were filled with rings, gold and silver. I loved her eyes, though I feared them. One was almost black, the other a golden brown. And one of them, Grandpa had told me, Skarda could pull out and hold in her hand. An eye made of glass. I watched her from behind the coatrack, petting the fox, rubbing the eyes.

Babi got up to place two large pots of water on the stove to boil. Then she and Skarda went to the coal bin. As they passed the coatrack, a heavily ringed hand brushed past the fox fur and grabbed my wrist, snatching me from my hiding place. They both laughed and Babi rubbed my head as Skarda pulled me into the coal bin with them. From a pocket somewhere in her skirt she took a piece of hot red candy and pushed it past my lips. And then she kissed each of my eyes and whispered words of another language in my ear. There was a scent of Babi's backyard flowers about her. I pictured roses. Without quite understanding it I felt, for the first time, desire wrapped in fear. I had no language for it but silence and the senses.

Babi pulled the light chain in the coal bin while Skarda closed the wooden door behind us. The two of them continued to talk, and then Skarda, lifting the burlap bag in one hand, gestured for me to take out a chicken. She guided my hand partway in till I felt a jabbing pain as something clamped my finger, and I pulled back crying.

Taking my hand to her lips, Skarda kissed it. Holding my head in the crook of her arm, she wiped my eyes with her shawl. Not until I had calmed down, not until Babi had pulled the ax free from the

chopping stump and run her thumb over the edge, did Skarda release the first chicken, untying its leathery yellow claws and handing it to Babi.

It was beautiful and white; its neck curved up in a bright red comb as it twisted to right itself, its tiny eye seeming to hold us all in question. Babi quickly grabbed and held the wing and half the bird in one hand, settling it on the block like a bundle, continually nudging its neck with the head of the ax, murmuring to it to behave and lie still.

And in that second of stillness, when the feathered neck stopped writhing and the eye of the chicken blinked a moment of calm, Babi brought down the ax in a thud, a cry close to joy in her voice, and quickly stepped back to let the headless chicken bleed clean in its crazed dance around the coal bin, Skarda and Babi laughing and swaying amid the whirring wings and flying feathers. They waited till the feathers and the coal dust settled, till the body of the bird seemed to lodge itself and expire upon the coal pile. Then Skarda urged me with a slight push to go bring it to her. Crouched low within reach, I studied the slow flow of blood that pumped from its neck. Extending a hesitant hand to its claws, I touched the bird slightly, bringing it furiously to life for an instant, blood and feathers on my hand. I heard myself join into the laughter of the women and, wrapped into the arms of Skarda, saw it all happen before my eyes again.

Babi brushed the black dust from the white feathers with the backs of her fingers, extinguished the light, and carried all three of the chickens into the kitchen, holding them in one hand by the claws, dropping them into the boiling pots of water to

SKARDA

loosen the feathers, dipping them in and out quickly, two or three times.

   Seated at the table with the wet chickens, Skarda and Babi pulled feathers till the skin shone white with a cast of blue. Reaching for the knife under the table, Babi slit an opening in the end of each chicken, stuffed her whole hand in the cavity, and pulled out handfuls of slippery innards. She pinched the heart free and pushed it toward me. She held tiny yellow nodules in her fingers, explaining to me that these were eggs and all of this would be turned into soup. Skarda pointed to the iridescent blue of the gizzard, which looked like a jewel for a ring on one of her fingers.
   When the chickens were washed and prepared, when the soup was set on the stove to cook, when the coffee cups were filled and the table cleaned of feathers, Skarda and Babi sat down to their game of cards. And though Skarda still frightened me, she caught my attention with the black silk pouch she removed from her bag, and I sat in her lap as she showed me the cards.
   There was a tower on fire with people falling out; there was a man pushing a boat with swords sticking up from the bottom; there was a woman pouring water near a pond with stars all around her; there was a skeleton riding a white horse, a man hanging upside down, another man about to walk off a cliff; and in all of them I saw stories. I was the child riding the horse on a card of the sun. I pictured myself hanging upside down. I was pushing across the water with people in a boat stuck with swords. And these were all like dreams but still as real as the basement, the at-

tic, the flat, Babi, Grandpa, and me.

The coffee cups were removed, the table wiped clean. Skarda held the deck in her hand, picked a card with a woman seated between two columns, one black and one white, with the moon at her feet, and set it down. Babi moved her chair close to her as Skarda shuffled the deck, cut it three times, tapped all the cards into place, and centered the deck on the table. She placed a ringed and jeweled hand upon them, said some words, and Babi's hand came down upon hers. Then Skarda took my hand and put it on top of theirs.

Around the card she had first chosen for Babi, Skarda slowly turned over more cards in the pattern of a triangle. It was very quiet in the basement except for the noise of the stove and Babi talking to herself when the pictures appeared on the cards. Three times she brought down her fist on the table and cursed: the card with the heart pierced by three swords; the picture of a woman sitting up in bed who seemed to be crying in the midst of swords hanging over her head; and the skeleton riding the white horse, which bothered her most of all. She put her hands to her mouth, muffling a short scream.

Skarda said nothing for a long while. She tapped and studied the card with a picture of the moon. She carefully moved her hands to other cards, tapping the sun, the fool, as if to include them, then whispered to Babi, tapping my hand at the same time, clutching it, giving the moon to me. The afternoon passed in whispers.

Skarda left as it began to get dark. I could see a light snow beginning to fall on the back steps as she closed the door behind her. I wondered where I

SKARDA

would sleep that night, the first time I would be staying over at Babi's, and when Grandpa would be coming home. The pots on the stove, the oven, occupied Babi's attention. She continued to talk to herself. I found paper and pencil and tried drawing some of the pictures from Skarda's cards. Babi pulled the picture of the skeleton from me, slapped my hand, gathered all of the crude sketches before me, and put them into the fire.

She put a soup bowl before me, ladled all three of the hearts into it, and told me to eat, all the while scolding me about the pictures. I broke the pencil when she was not looking, threw it under the table, ate one heart, and left the rest of the soup. She buttered a piece of bread for me, but I would not eat it. She poured a glass of milk, and I let it stand. She raised her hand as if to hit me, and I fled to the front basement. I touched the drums, which I was forbidden to touch. I went back behind the furnace to see the goldfish that Babi had placed in a large metal tub for winter. Their color had all but disappeared in the darkness of the basement. I felt around in the water with my hand, trying to catch one and bring it to the light to see if the color was still there.

Later, Babi and I played bunco, waiting for Grandpa to come home. Anger began to crackle from her in different tongues. She was angry at the dice, angry at Grandpa, at Skarda, and even at me for not eating, for having to stay with her the whole day and now the night.

The basement door opened. The whole side of Grandpa from his fur cap to his foot was packed in a ghostly imprint of snow. He had fallen in the gangway near the gate.

THE GHOST OF SANDBURG'S PHIZZOG

Babi hurried him into a chair and immediately language erupted from both of them, and I fled to the coatrack in terror. Grandpa's face was bleeding. As his voice subsided, Babi continued to goad him while removing his coat, wiping his face and hands, and finally kneeling before him to unlace his shoes.

She set a bowl of soup in front of him, cut and then buttered his bread. She cursed and turned away from him, banging pots on the stove, then hurled a hot lid at him. He reached under the table for the butcher knife and came after her, into the front basement, around the furnace, back into the kitchen, and to the door leading upstairs. She looked for the key, but it was missing. Grandpa flung the knife at her and fell. The wooden handle bounced off the fat of her upper arm.

Again she helped him into his chair, set a whole roast chicken on a platter before him, a carving knife and a fork, poured him a glass of beer, then mumbled and motioned toward his pocket for the ring of keys.

What happened to the one I tied to the doorknob that's supposed to be there? he shouted mostly in English and a few words in Czech.

Babi didn't know. It was there this morning.

Skarda! Grandpa cursed. She makes you crazy. She'll come back sometimes and take the whole upstairs and you won't know. You don't watch her. She'll steal you blind. Here, here, he handed her the key. Give it back. Go to bed. Where's the boy?

Talking to herself, she opened the door, turned halfway around, and flung the ring of keys at his head. He cursed her again, throwing his fork, striking her leg as she lumbered upstairs.

Come here, he hollered toward me. I see you.

SKARDA

I came toward him very slowly from my hiding place, fearful of being hit or killed with the knife he poked into the chicken and into his mouth.

Up here, he said, pulling me onto his lap. He smelled of fragrant backyard flowers, the same as Skarda. And whiskey. And blood. He sliced thin pieces of crisp chicken and told me to chew hard. He speared hunks of meat with the point of the knife, placed them on my tongue, and showed me how to draw them off the blade between my teeth. He held a glass of cold beer to my lips and told me to sip.

Did she take your eyes? he touched them with a finger and a thumb. Did Skarda steal your heart? he hugged the breath out of me and laughed.

Make a wish, he said, tearing the breastbone from the chicken and handing me half. We pulled till it cracked—the wish was to be mine. Then he took me upstairs to bed.

There was no light, yet we could see. Holding his hand, I followed him through the upstairs kitchen to a door, a lock, a key, and another flight of stairs leading to the attic, where I had never been before. We burrowed through the cold darkness ribbed with rafters, across creaking floorboards, past trunks and boxes covered in white sheets, and into a small room in front with slanted walls and two windows, blue in the winter light.

There was a bed in one corner, a cedar chest against the wall that I could smell, and one chair. I quickly undressed. Grandpa lifted the *pesina*, holding it in the air, while I crawled in and felt it float down upon me like a cloud. Two feather pillows were fluffed beneath my head. He patted my cheek, the scent of Skarda still on his hand, leaving me with

that and his footsteps departing across the creaking floor. Three days later, working in the icehouse, he would fall over dead.

I watched the light in the windows a long time. I listened. The house upstairs seemed to sway. I awoke sometime later to a scream—my own?—my heart pounding, my body trembling. My face frozen, yet beneath the feather comforter my body curled in a warmth close to fire. I could not see. Skarda had stolen my eyes. They would not open, and I began to cry. Slowly the tears dissolved the crust that had accumulated along the lids. I spread them open with my fingers, slipped out of bed, and made my way through the cold toward the steps leading downstairs.

I reached the first floor and heard what sounded like a sigh. Both Babi and Grandpa were asleep in the house somewhere, surely far removed from my thoughts for now. I was alone. And all this belonged to me.

I went down to the basement and rubbed my eyes with cold water in the sink. I fed bread crumbs from the table to the goldfish and listened for them to move in the water. I turned the light on in the coal bin, walked to the front of the basement, and plugged in the lights to Uncle Frankie's drum. It blossomed in colors of rose, gold, and green. I gave the foot pedal a solid thump.

Starting back upstairs to bed, I remembered the coatrack, turned, and came down the stairs again to rummage in the pockets of my jacket. I felt the key on the string. I found the eye I had removed from Skarda's fox.

SKARDA

Opening the furnace door, I threw in the key and watched the string ignite in the flames. I took the eye of Skarda's fox upstairs with me to bed.

My room in the attic was so white that I thought the roof had disappeared and snow had fallen in. The two windows were blind with an intricacy of frost that spoke of backyard gardens, images suspended in a dream wanting to be made real. If I pressed too close with my hand, it would melt and disappear into the moon beyond. I found my old hollow warmth under the *pesina*. I clutched Skarda's eye for safekeeping.

In the Secret Places
Of the Stairs

Pritzker, everyone's man-of-the-hour, any hour, at the Hardwaren Apartments. Pritzker downstairs in the boiler room, rising from his cot. Wilma on the edge, pulling up her pants.

That was good, lover, she says. You really fixed me. I can stand on my sore feet again, corns, calluses, fallen arches and all. I can carry the weight of all the trays of dirty dishes in the world in these hands, dump them into the sink without a sound. But I'd rather hold on to your pumping hard ass. Here, fix me.

A bent hook, Wilma. Let me straighten it.

Pritzker, unshaven, prickly, angling for those wrinkled orange lips, the slight wisp of hair upon her upper lip. An almost old man, sixty three, half asleep, kissing an almost old woman reeking of gift perfume. A working woman of customary pleasures, married, living in the same building he services. A waitress with bad feet. A stop-gap love. A patch-job repair at best.

What's to be fixed, Pritzker? Something old for good, or something new for a change? Ula, from the old country, needs help. Surely a man is entitled to some innocence in the dark golden years, a lifetime of parts breaking down?

Bending the hook back into shape with his fingers, holding her coarse tongue between his teeth ... he feels the time ... considers the act maybe just preventive maintenance. Her hair in his hands gently, the same color and feel of packing straw he pulled from a refrigerator crate yesterday.

He strains, lifts, rocks the heaviness of her over ripe and yellowing ass ... Wilma ... Wilma ... Wilma ... God speaks of second chances ... What's

to be denied? Whispering in her ear to himself, swallowing his own words.

That tickles, she says, grabbing his rough cheeks, plunging a tongue into his mouth to stop his breath.

Your husband Althoff, he mumbles. He's clogging my system. I must live with him too. Your place is cold again he tells me. I've got a job to do.

All my life I've been married to a man who can do nothing, says Wilma, stuffing herself into her garments. Leave bad enough alone. I can handle it. I'm all sympathy, even for you, lonely man. You believe me? In sickness or health, for better or even worse. Service, he loves. Even sickness is satisfactory. Do anything for him ... he'll kill you with kindness. But I'd marry you tomorrow, fix-it-man, till death do us part.

Death did his part with my Violet, three years ago, mumbles Pritzker. It was not very memorable—the life I mean. Married thirty-eight years to a woman with a bad heart the last fifteen. Some people are born with heart trouble. The diets, the doctors, the pills, the high blood pressures, the "this is not good for my heart" business ... the suffering was mostly mine. Bad news—most people make a life of it. If your Althoff knew about us, he'd probably feel better. Tell him.

What do you want, Pritzker? You want that young one on the roof?

Want, want, want ... what's *want?* I'm *want*. Me. Everybody wants Pritzker. I want my body to work like before again. The head I'll keep. You want a husband. You got one. Keep him. And me too, if you want. Only don't ask questions when you know the answers.

IN THE SECRET PLACES OF THE STAIRS

You bastard. That's not what I want. Come here, lover ...

Althoff? He knows what's going on down here?

No. I lie, Pritzker. I lie. What's going on?

You're all simple moving parts, Wilma. Well oiled, well worn. No complexity. You'll last forever.

It works. You believe me? ... I love you, handyman ... grabbing hold of him, pinching with her broken red fingernails till he howls in real and pretended pain. Getting into her uniform, her shoes ... Oh my goddam aching feet ... drifting a little to the left, just a hair off plumb in his eyes, as she approaches the door with a backside soliloquy: I hate a self-service man. Smacking him a goodbye kiss with her hand.

What do you want out of life, lover? she asks, turning the latch.

Drama, he says.

You've got it, kiddo, she exits in laughter, blinking away the tears.

I'll take that too! he shouts at her laughing footsteps rising and fading on the concrete stairwell. And something new! he continues hollering. A different job, maybe selling things like frost-free refrigerators, self-cleaning ovens, maintenance-free furnaces! Something new, lowering his voice, talking to himself ... a young woman again ... searching with bare feet under the cot for socks and shoes. No pain, he whispers ... no history.

Pritzker dressed and tied bundles of old newspapers to feed the furnace, feeling a wave of fire and a new day in his bones. Veteran of a double hernia, heartburn, hemorrhoids, and the painful signs of arthritic joints ... the body, nevertheless,

THE GHOST OF SANDBURG'S PHIZZOG

rising from the ashes again with the poking and shaking, the hard handling of Wilma. Not to be denied either. But purring now with the images of young Ula upstairs, the cousin of a cousin from the other side, near Vilna, shuffled here amongst distant relatives in the city, like a misplaced part. Finally dumped into his hands just three days ago by his brother, Morris, with simple instructions: You want her maybe in the building. To help? Which Pritzker reads as: Keep. Maybe a replacement for Violet. A brand new heart. Ah, the mixed blessings God bestows upon us. Job, what were you waiting for? Such a do-nothing!

Pritzker? No questions asked. I fix. Pritzker, the man known to all others as one who can do things. To make them work again. To put the right washer in the kitchen faucet. To take the ball of hair out of the gooseneck in the bathroom sink. Pritzker, primed with the red plunger or the plumber's snake coiled in his hand ready to dislodge whatever evil in the world has seized the draining system.

Pritzker rummaging through a warped workbench drawer for a file to clean and pick his nails. Wrenches, hammers, broken screwdrivers, a ring of red rubber washers, bits, pliers, wire, springs.... There is no order in the universe of tool drawers. What you're looking for is never where it is. Where it is, is wrong.

Pritzker, where are you? Pritzker, you sure can fix things.

Knock, knock, knock ... Pritzker? Pritzker, please come fix my bowl ... knock, knock, knock. When I flushed this morning, the water never came back again to the rusty ring mark like it's supposed

IN THE SECRET PLACES OF THE STAIRS

to. It just sits a little bit at the bottom. Looks funny, such a big white bowl so empty. I'm afraid to sit on it. Knock, knock, knock ... Do you hear, Pritzker?

Don't flush till I get there ... Pritzker primping, humming. Lathering the cheeks, the jowls ... running the safety edge razor around and over the Adam's apple. Rinsing, dabbing, rubbing redness into his cheeks with an off-white towel, scratchy in too many places. Plunging his thumb along the teeth of a black plastic comb. Knots and falling hair ... a part, a slight wave ... there now, there.

Up to the penthouse first to see Ula ... untouched by Pritzker, repairer, mender, mechanic with years of grease imbedded in his hands. Not that she should be soiled by me, become worn. Little Ula, up to his chest, measuring her life in his head till his groin springs alive with visions of innovations. Nineteen years old and already a slight roughness of scrubwoman knees. No stairs for her in his building. No floors. Mops, sponges, no twisting of sodden wet rags by hand. Rubber gloves.

Pritzker rising to the heights of the third floor stairwell, catching a breath, ascending slowly to the fifth floor and beyond ... the roof, the heavenly penthouse put together for her out of the shed-like storage place near the chimney.

For Violet, he turned it into a greenhouse of sorts before the bad heart business set in and the raising of high blood pressure by stairs. Leaving Pritzker oh so suddenly alone with a greenhouse ... a maintenance man to flowers and plants of all sorts. Soft machinery. Science fiction to his ten oily thumbs.

What do you mean, the seedlings are "damping off"? he screams at a wife with an irregular heart

beat. How do you fix a fucking begonia to bloom?

Days and nights adjusting sun, adjusting water, adjusting earth. What verities these, to a man with a screwdriver? None of the plants responding for him but the mother-in-law's tongue, *sansevieria*, snake plant, which he knows grows with indifference, even hate, surviving eternities of neglect in the windows of barbershops.

They die, die. All of you bastards impossible to keep going in Pritzer's hands. Locking the door to the greenhouse forever, six months before Violet's heart pumped its final beat.

You are a murderer, she said.

Yes, I am that too, no doubt. Guilty but not guilty. Some things should be left alone. Like plants. God did not make me responsible for the propagation of German ivy.

In love and anger, dropping flats and flower pots from the roof to the alley below like bombs, the day after her funeral. In remorse, in the emptiness, saving only the snake plant for a dark shelf of the boiler room, thriving on electric light and Pritzker's contempt. Grow, he sneered. No help from me.

Then gutting the inside of the greenhouse, sufocating in stale sunlight, opening windows to rid the room of the deadly smell of soil ... the grave ... the ghost of Violet. Filling it first with broken doors and oven racks, washing machine motors and spare parts. Months, it takes months, sweats Pritzker, for the natural odor of oil and grease, the comfort of storage to settle and make a place habitable for a man once again.

With the announcement of Ula ... Pritzker builds a penthouse. Out with the old, in with the new. New

IN THE SECRET PLACES OF THE STAIRS

chairs, new table, new rug, new sofa bed. Fresh paint on the walls and a glad heart. She is new only in not meeting him, he understands. Knowing, as he does, the dreams of those from the other side ... all of them wanting only discovery. Columbuses all. Place, work, and the money to make things different. Pritzker would provide a new world up here. God would man the boiler room, as usual.

The last step to the sky ... the outside world and a door. Enter before knocking. Respecting his own right of way, Pritzker closes the door behind him, knocking gently on the inside. Ula standing at the table, a confusion and sadness about her. Two white cups and saucers, a matching set of yellow plastic sugar bowl and creamer. Bread in her hands for the toaster. Coffee perking ... objects all of domesticity ... a small part of the world that works, when the heart is in it. My God, thinks Pritzker, she could be a wife!

She pours silver, it seems, from a shiny electric percolator. Pritzker thinks, nodding his thanks, patting her perfectly bent elbow. Such a soft arm he wants turned and tightened around him. A wrist to bend freely and kiss ... such hands and loving fingers ... No sign of the blue wired veins, the knots of Wilma's flesh and joints. Near Ula, his own aches dissolve.

Today is easy, he begins. Nothing. You should maybe shop, look around the neighborhood. Some money ... here, twenty dollars. Putting her at ease. Next week, an empty apartment to do, floors to clean, walls to wash. You help me. Just watch. No hurry. A leaky elbow under the sink for me to fix. An outlet to replace.

THE GHOST OF SANDBURG'S PHIZZOG

A quizzical expression on her face. Elbow? Outlet? Laughingly, a debonair Pritzker waving his hand, of no concern to you, he comforts her. Ula buttering toast, mixing milk and sugar in his coffee. Let me, taking the spoon from her. No need to wait on hand and foot. Just a friendly visit.

The woman downstairs, he explains... Krava, old lady Krava's waiting for me. Broken toilet. No water. Always a plumbing problem with her. Then Althoff, third floor rear. My hot-air expert. No heat again. There's heat. It's only Althoff. Hot and cold is a mystery to him.

Ula rising to pour more coffee... Pritzker reaching to resist her services... no, let me, he gestures, wresting the pot free, only to lose it between them, crashing to the table, burning their hands in scalding coffee.

Pritzker rushing her to the sink, running cold water over the fingers. Cursing the burn, feeling the fool. Grabbing a stick of butter from the table, rubbing it over the red tenderness of her pain, suffering in silence his own finger on fire. Sitting her on the sofa then, holding her hand. A warm wateriness about her eyes... a feeling to fix. Blister, he tells her. You don't want a blister. Pritzker petting the hair on her head.

She, realizing again her own trap of dependencies in a new world, living them through almost unknowningly with a strength of expression manifested only in wiles... Ula moving to discourage the undeserved attention. *My* clumsiness, *my* inexperience... not yours.

But Pritzker forcing his own right to ignorance, stupidity, guilt in her eyes, her hands. And Ula, the

child, the woman, accepting, raising her hurt and his hand together to his lips for the loving absolution of his kisses. Pritzker on fire, exchanging fingers for lips, for awkward kisses, for the warm hollow of her mouth.

Then easing her down alongside him on the sofa until hands and arms are free, lock the open space between them ... forcing, resisting ... her head shaking off a flurry of no's and a soft weeping.

Pritzker letting go, bolting from the penthouse ... fool, fool, what an old fool! ... flapping down the stairs, the unmaking of a handyman faced with the strength of innocence: the old standby. My own undoing. If such a man be fool enough, call him Pritzker. Nursing his own burnt finger in his mouth. Stealing buttered kisses from a child! Robbing the cradle, robbing the grave. Oh, Violet, with a glad heart made for dying. Oh, Wilma, old warhorse, can you blame this Solomon of the sweatshop wanting to sing anew? What's to be left undone? Controls are for heating systems, not men just past their prime.

Pritzker, standing in reverence before old lady Krava's empty bowl, fixing, staring, waiting for the oracle to speak. Flush ... *the cistern contains: the fountain overflows ...*

I told you it doesn't work, she says.

It works, it works ... patience. You see this burning finger? Throbbing in little circles, hard and soft, hard and soft? Do you know what the prophets see? That's what begins to play hide and seek with me. You can see God in a monkey wrench, if you handle it right.

How do you fix it so it won't break again, Pritzker?

THE GHOST OF SANDBURG'S PHIZZOG

Pritzker dousing his hot finger in the toilet tank ... ahh ... adjusting the float. Flush, down and up, gurgle, the in and out rushing of water alive in the bowl. The beautiful equilibrium of the ball float, leveling Pritzker momentarily in a clear water sigh of grace mechanically produced, deserved.

Such drama taking place in a body, my own finger, who knows about not breaking again? Rejoice! Your bowl is full once more. Sit. Reflect. Keep your eye on the watermark.

Mounting the stairs again toward Ula, two-at-a-time, two-at-a-time, the confusion of forgiveness heavy on the heart. Humming to find the words ... I am sorry? You are sorry? It is sorry? For what? For nothing. For accepting her here? Setting her up with intent to desire? Love? Preserve?

Knock, knock, knock ... Ula? Silence. Ula? Rattle, rattle, a locked door. All the keys to the world hanging from Pritzker's belt, but he will not enter.

Put more butter on the burn, he advises her, his lips pressed against the door. Run cold water over it. Ula, hear me? I fixed old lady Krava's toilet. Nothing serious. If you like, dust the windowsills in the hall- ways. Use the other hand. Ula? Does it hurt? Tell me if it's all right.... Tell me the truth.

Pritzker, Pritzker, order in the universe. Down to the third floor rear to check on Althoff's radiator. You got a burning finger, Althoff's got a bad radiator. And a bad wife to boot. Punishment ... a malfunction in the system. Correctable.

You fixed his wife's bra this morning, and she was grateful, she was good. She's always good. A nice, maybe perfect woman on your hands. Still, I love you, you can't say to her. The words don't come out.

IN THE SECRET PLACES OF THE STAIRS

The feeling, the apparatus, broken down after a lifetime of Violet. I love you, fuel for the passions of youth. With age, you don't advertise. You make amends. You use what still works ... and should be satisfied. But with Ula ... now the possibilities of a young heart once again. To mean to say I love you, for sure, for the first time in forty years. Improbable fixings for a Pritzker. But I will lay down my tools before the powers of the universe to see it happen.

Wilma and Althoff, Pritzker knows how it works between them. How they fight since he lost his voice and lost his balls. Seal it already, Pritzker. Tie it up. Explain to Althoff how a waitress makes a chancy wife. A waitress dishes out only herself ... servings of eyes, hands, tits, legs, ass. All dessert. Make him believe. He can fix it.

Turn up the heat. Turn on the lights. Who needs a piece of Wilma for nourishment more than Althoff? Mark off a spot on her rear end with electrician's tape. Tell him there are simple things any man can do. Show him where to plant his foot. Or maybe his lips? Althoff?

come in ... come in ... jesus, pritzker, where's the heat? ... the radiator hasn't bubbled all day ... i've been home long enough to know when the heat comes ... it comes in trickles, pritzker ... during the day it hardly comes at all ... at night, around the six o'clock news ... the bubbling begins to build ... then about the time Wilma should come home, all of a sudden there's this burst of heat that lasts till the ten o'clock news ... then it disappears again.

That's because you got air in your radiator, Althoff. I told you you got to drain the radiator, got to bleed it regularly or else all that air builds up. That's

THE GHOST OF SANDBURG'S PHIZZOG

what all the bubbling's about. Air, Althoff! You got to understand circulation. Get me an empty can or something. Let me show you for the last time. That's why I left the little key for you. You put that key in here, and you turn the valve just a little like this, and it starts bleeding ... pssssssssstttttt ... gguurrrrrgggllleee ... Hear? Like an upset stomach. See? Air, Althoff. Then comes the water. But first the bad air. It blocks the heat. Here, try it yourself ... Good, good. See, you can do it.

 thank you, pritzker ... thank you ...

 You got to learn to live with hot water, Althoff. How's the chords? When do you start talking like you got some balls again?

 the doctor says it'll take eighteen months ... he cut right in here, you see? right around the vocal chords ... then he went in there and stretched them ... hurt like hell ... can't go back to work for a least another three months ... it's up to Wilma to bring home the bacon now ... ha, ha, ha, ...

 If that's all she brings home, you'll be all right, Althoff.

 don't say that, pritzker ... she's a good wife ... i trust her ...

 I know Althoff. I do too.

 we've been married too long for any monkey business ... she doesn't even know how to lie ... she comes in at midnight, goes out again to relax ... she's in and out all day ... it's a tough job, on your feet so many hours ... don't tell me she chases.

 No, maybe she's getting too old to chase, Althoff. What's a woman her age, her shape, going to chase? We limp along, don't we, Althoff? Teeth fall out, the body begins to sag, the plumbing is undependable ...

IN THE SECRET PLACES OF THE STAIRS

things dry up, break, lose color, wear out. But still...
    and there's comfort in that, pritzker, comfort... i am not a religious man, but even with this throat operation i feel better about everything ... it's just something else a man can't do a thing about ... but Wilma, i swear she must think she's got forever ... you want to know a little secret? she's all gray ... white, as a matter of fact. she spends hours making herself up, and she's sixty years old, prtizker. Sixty ... close up, you can't tell. if you seen what i see, ha, ha, ha, you can tell. but sometimes in the bedroom, watching her in the mirror, i want to shut off the light and jump her, she seems so young and beautiful. ah, well, that's life. those days are over, as my father used to say. what's the matter with your finger, pritzker? looks like you're going to end up with a blister on your hand.

Just a burn. I'm learning to live with it. I have to wait to see how it heals, Althoff. You got to learn to live all over again with pain. Deny it exists, if you can. The pain won't let you forget. It's hard to fix in a man's mind, but the human body is a marvelous machine... What do we all want, Althoff? Another chance ... another chance.

Pritzker, downstairs at the workbench in the boiler room, late in the day. Repairing a light switch, reaching for the loud wind-up alarm clock minus the big hand ... winding it, shaking it, propping it up against the back of the workbench just to hear it tick.

Time is a big thing, hums Pritzker, taking up a screwdriver numbly against the blistered finger, the whispering going on in his head. More important than talk. Talk is worse than cheap. Talk is nothing. To understand the kind of time it takes a finger to

heal... the burning, the blistering, the peeling away of the old skin for new... the whole process. A real timepiece—a woman. To set yourself on that... only that.

Pritzker tossing the light switch on the table... It's fixed. Famous last words... chisel them on my tombstone. Everything shoud be that simple... Nails pounding themselves into wood, pipes threading into each other minus the agony of the wrench. All should have the silence, the smoothness of blood. The on and off flow of light... energy... electricity through a mercury switch. Just a touch of a finger. To come and go like that.

Pritzker stuffing the long screwdriver in a drawer, taking it out again as he spies the snake plant in the corner... setting it down before him, turning over the earth with the screwdriver. Administering a pipethumping shot of cold water from the faucet... leaves awash and shiny green again... new shoots all around. No thanks to me, says Pritzker.

Destination: penthouse. Pritzker on the backsteps going up, early in the evening, holding the newly potted snake plant against his chest, rehearsing forgiveness without end with each step... Ula, for you, please. Force is what gets things done for me. Not natural. I natural. I'm sorry....

Now finding himself before her without the words coming... the door locked... taking the matter into his own hands, opening the door with his own set of keys, putting the plant down on the table. You don't do anything to it, it lives, he says softly to her. She, sitting on the sofa, a white dish rag wrapped around part of her hand, sewing buttons on a sweater, fastening her eyes on the old man's awkward steps.

IN THE SECRET PLACES OF THE STAIRS

Pritzker smiling on one knee, losing his balance, taking her hand, undoing the rag, blowing on the burn. No bandage, understand? It will take care of itself. It needs to breathe ... must have fresh air. A whole different system of fixing. Pritzker kissing the burn gently. I have some salve downstairs. I'll bring you up some salve.

Rising on both legs, easing himself beside her on the edge of the sofa. The scent of Wilma from the morning still upon him ... an old calling card. Does it hurt? Ula nodding no. Good ... good. It will get better for you. Everything. Ula taking her hand back slowly.

Breaking the thread in her teeth, spreading the sweater with the new buttons on her knee, placing the needle between her lips. Pritzker removing it, sticking it into the arm of the sofa.

I will find you another place, some other work, Pritzker explaining, taking her hand again, talking to her hand in his ... afraid of her eyes. Maybe back near my brother. People there will help you, look after you, maybe find you a young man. Work, marry, go on with it.

Ula pressing his hand in hers, feeling the pain, touching her lips to him in thanks, without thought.

Pritzker feeling for her again amidst the ashes, mindful of the morning, the pain, but still wanting the fullness, the nakedness he slowly makes of her, the coolness now sliding under him. Kissing the unblemished tautness of her body spreading out so before his hands ... the reticence of things untried. Pritzker at his clumsiest, on his feet, undoing his own clothes, falling from him true-to-form....

And now you have the man, praise God, standing

nakedly above her. Approaching ... but taken aback to see her arms rise suddenly, miraculously above her, to see her witnessing for the first time, powers within herself ... fingers waving, eyes working ... in passion? ... in wonder? ... in pain? ... in love? ... in falseheartedness? Beckoning him with a force far back in time, surprising them both with the endless new certainties. Entangling Pritzker in his own first steps ... inverting the man in place. Hot-footing it back into his clothes again, fitting comfortably, perfectly, beyond a doubt.

Pritzker settling downstairs toward the boiler room like a falling leaf. Fumbling in the dark for the light chain. Undressing, washing in the cement basin. Lathering the face, the arms, the chest, the hands, the fingers. Running the hot, the cold water. Accepting the lukewarm. Drying the burnt finger well.

Pritzker asleep, stretched out on his cot. Hands joined behind his head, fingers in perfect peace. Legs spread out. The wheezing, the breathing unending. A slight hum.

Wilma coming in toward morning, shedding her uniform. Climbing on top of him. Lying flat, positioning the hollows, the bones, the swellings, the scars, the bruises, the contours of two bodies for comfort. Locking the feet for flight. First encircling his neck, then taking his arms, extending them, his hands, his fingers, beyond the confines of the cot. A pleasurable cross of no bearing. A lofty possibility of wings.

Kissing him. Speaking in silent tongues. Settling between his legs, rubbing, scratching their parts together for the fusion, the fire, the certain fit of a long moving life.

IN THE SECRET PLACES OF THE STAIRS

We tighten, we loosen, we work wonderously, whispers Pritzker, absorbing her in the abondonment of his dreams. We're fixed for good.

An American Presence

Frozen in Sharkey's memory ...

A melody, a line, a question:

Which side are you on, boy? Which side are you on? Like so many mindless Hail Marys and Our Fathers sounding through him on Sunday mornings. Whistling it through his teeth now, steadying himself before a gilt-framed mirror in the living room. Fixing his blue overseas cap—Past Commander—at an angle long remembered. Courage, confidence, commitment. Still a touch of the old salt about him.

Which side are you on, boy? "Are you comin' with me?" Nudging Chuckie's leg off the hassock. The silence of an only son asleep, adrift in the ghostly blue images of an old movie on television. Long-haired, mustachioed, an empty beer bottle stuck between his thighs, Zig Zag cigarette papers scattered on his lap. Sweet smoke.

Sharkey rearranging the venetian blinds. A light snow filtering past the ever-brightening street lamp. Blocking it all out. Closing the blinds. Dropping them with a crash upon the windowsill. Sharkey uncomfortable in the silence.

Lance Corporal Charles Korczak, Fifth Marine Regiment, Delta Company, rifleman, twitching, stirring awake. Hue City, the battle of the Citadel, crack shot, 96 confirmed, 15 months in 'Nam. Home again. "It's like ice in here. You got a window open? Going where?"

"The Legion with me."

Which side are you on, boy? Depending on whether you sit, stand, shout, salute ... first in war, first in peace ... "Legion," a fireworks of red, white, and blue feelings ... a semaphore of silent satire.

THE GHOST OF SANDBURG'S PHIZZOG

Chaplinesque. Chuckie grinning at the sight of his old man: parade rest. But ready. Peace.

Pacification programs ... American advisers, observers .. S-2's good-will programs, "helping" the villagers. The CIA with soul. The Lance Corporal pulled back, assigned as a radio operator with S-2, assisting an American adviser in pacifying the villagers. Bringing soap and cigarettes, helping the helpless. First you find the village elder ... who leads the American adviser to a booby-trapped hut. Good riddance. Good will. Which side are you on, boy? The Lance Corporal exchanging roles within himself, assuming attitude of unofficial American observer, taking the whole scene a few yards back, sighting it through an M-16. Bringing down the village elders ... first.

"Either you're comin' or you're not," says Sharkey. "You don't have to join. I'm not tellin' you to join. Stay home. Be another long-haired peace freak like the rest of them Viet vets. Dopeheads."

The unofficial American observer smiling secretly in his stretching ... casting:

cut to ...

Elliot Gould, maybe, in Boy Scout uniform sending distress signals, whirling two fists of flags, calling a Legion of three big-bellied men to acute attention ...

or

... a handful of middle-aged legionnaires in blue-and-gold overseas caps standing at a bar, reliving WWII stories, while two WWI vets sit quietly at a table staring at a deck of cards. Storytellers, patriots, Americans all.

"Maybe next week, Shark. I want to catch the late movie, a Western."

"Don't be a deadass. Screw those old movies. That's all you do every night. There's only one old movie I'd ever want to see again: *The Best Years of Our Lives*. I was crying for crissake when I saw it. Come on. If your ma was alive, if she was here, she'd get you to go. She wouldn't let you just sit here on your ass. Come on. The guys want to know what you're up to, what it was like."

Chuckie Korczak gathering the loose cigarette papers on his lap. The Lance Corporal retired. The unofficial American observer, just moving along peaceful like, driving through a dead-end job of no sweat, installing for the Victor Window Shade & Blind Company. A sign painted boldly on the back of his delivery van: CAUTION BLIND MAN DRIVING. Leaving his bumper-conscious countrymen behind him with a laugh.

"They want to know about that slant-eyed stuff you were gettin' over there."

"Tell them the Thai women were ... ah, hell, Shark, I can't describe them. Tell them I wished I could have brought one home for a souvenir, like your Japanese sword."

"Well, come on and just talk about that Thai-women stuff."

The Thai woman, he would like to explain. Ai Pa Ma ... and such sweet thighs. A Bangkok beauty of such translucent loveliness he was never quite certain of how much time with her passed. He was certain of nothing but the missing $200 when he awoke. And the poem.

Ai Pa Ma ... porcelain, gold silk thighs wrapped around every part of him, clutching and rocking his head in gentleness, midnight hair sweeping and teas-

ing his lips. Afternoons on the riverfront, the Temple of the Fig Tree, the chapel of the Reclining Buddha. Ai Pa Ma leading the Lance Corporal by hand through a city that glowed.

Opium evenings of her stretched out in a kimono of black and gold. Nights of the soft bells of Bangkok. The war ending with a blood-stained uniform shed in the corner. That for this, cradling him inside her arms, the darkness of her unspoken history for the emptiness of hate instilled in a mother country. He thought it was love enfolded. He thought it was gone.

She taught him songs and poems, if she ever lived at all. Slant-eyed gash, the boys reminded him, all the same. She took the $200 and dissolved in an opium dream.

Strung out for days, the Lance Corporal, not even sure of her name, pulled back from the line again — five confirmed. All of them looking the same, though he searched for the slightest memory of an Eastern face. He had the poem in his head, that was all...

> Whose sleeves do you unfold
> While leaving me to lie here
> Night after night
> Alone on my widest robe?

"Shark, it's your club. No hard feelings. I'll have a beer with you when you get back. Look it here. Give me that cap. I mean, what the hell do I look like in this goddamn cap with long hair and everything? You see? You see? Even if I was serious, you'd have to laugh?"

AN AMERICAN PRESENCE

Sharkey smiling. Snatching the cap off his son's head, hitting him with it. "Well, maybe come on over anyway later for a drink."
The Lance Corporal saluting the Past Commander going out the door. Sharkey returning the gesture with a finger. Chuckie roaring his approval, returning the gesture, rolling another joint behind the closed door, lighting it, taking a long toke . . . sustaining images of the past.
cut to . . .
The Legion recalled . . . slot machines, beer, baseball, picnics, dances, parades, carnivals, essays on freedom, big-city conventions of grown men pinching women. God Bless America. Sharkey there, always where he's needed, no questions asked. Service.

Seaman Stanley Korczak, "Sharkey," 53, Streets and Sanitation Department, City of Chicago, Snow Command, salt-truck operator, spreading 50,000 tons of it last winter, now easing his way down the steps, across the street, making tracks, feeling the depth and density of the first fall of the white stuff under his feet.
Deadheading it down the last two blocks to the Arthur Schweiger American Legion Post #236. Visions of the orange plows, a convoy of them pushing out of the garages to meet the city's first heavy snowfall. A craving for emergencies. Getting ahead of the ice. Spreading the salt. Making things safe.
Sharkey approaching the post, checking it out by force of habit. A small frame building, suggestions of phony Colonial America going to dust. In need of paint and patronage. Sharkey will paint the whole

THE GHOST OF SANDBURG'S PHIZZOG

damn place himself next spring if he has to.

He unlocks the door, puts on the lights, arranges a few chairs. Wiping off the bar, opening a fresh bottle for a shot of Old Grand Dad. Moving to the front of the bar and waiting for the men to assemble. Watching himself in the mirror. Adjusting his cap. Standing tough, one foot on the rail, 235 pounds. A stomach covering his brass belt buckle.

Starting on the bottled beer. One dead soldier, two dead soldiers, three dead soldiers ... Sharkey lining the empties along the bar. Which side are you on, boy? A blue knit shirt, gray cuffed work pants, black pointed shoes worn at the heels, maroon socks hanging beneath the ankles. A face full, flushed, dead certain. The crisp overseas cap with Past Commander lettered along the side. Proud and tough. He waves a sharp hello in the mirror to the images of the men entering the hall behind him.

A Yank. A World War Two man. He knows he's history's own man. Pearl Harbor. The *Maryland*. "Victory" was a word as close to a man's inside as "love." Iwo Jima, Normandy, Hiroshima would always ring a bell. A remembrance of victory gardens, practice air raids, blue and gold stars in the window. "What do you say, boys?"

The men assembling. A few of them around the bar, others milling around the empty hall. Thumps on the back for Sharkey. Quick handshakes. Signs above the bar proclaiming: FAMOUS LAST WORDS OF THE ART SCHWEIGER AMERICAN LEGION POST #236 ... I'LL BE THERE! HOW THE HELL DID WE EVER WIN A WAR! KEEP SMILING

"That's the story of my life," says Sharkey to

AN AMERICAN PRESENCE

Taylor tending bar. "Keep smiling. Keep faith. Another beer here, Taylor."

Then a wiseass grin. A face in an old fatigue jacket creeping up behind him in the mirror. Sharkey pouring the fresh beer as steady as he can. He's seeing things. Lance Corporal Korczak reporting. Lookin' like some goddamn peace freak with a red headband for crissake, like a goddamn Indian. Pinchin' out the weed, stuffin' it into his pocket. Laughin' like he's caught me off guard.

"The only ones who can come in here is Legion members and their guests," Sharkey says to the image in the mirror. "You're my goddamn guest. Now take off that damn headgear and straighten up. Taylor, fellas, this here's my boy, Chuckie Korczak, from Vietnam. He can tell you all about it."

"Just an observer," smiles Chuckie. "Tell me, when does this meeting begin?"

"Anytime I say it does," explains Sharkey. "Around eight."

Chuckie taking an exaggerated reading from his watch. "You're late. Where the hell is everybody?"

"You're lookin' at 'em. Ten or twelve guys."

"The whole damn post?"

"The rest of the bastards never come. We got 200 paid members though. They just never show up. It's that goddamn TV, that's what it is."

"No Viet vets?"

"Naw, those bastards won't show either. It's a different army, different navy, different everything. Every year we open 15 free memberships for those Vietnam guys, I get their names and everything, I get a hold of 'em, and maybe one will show up for the first meetin' and then that's the end of him."

THE GHOST OF SANDBURG'S PHIZZOG

"Maybe more free memberships or something."

"Christ, we'd give 60 if we could get one of 'em! What the hell's the difference? The bastards still won't join. They think the Legion's a war organization. What the hell am I telling you? You know what your buddies think. Taylor! Two more beers here and a little firewater. Take off that goddamn Indian thing, will you. And the jacket. What the hell did you do with the stripes?"

"It keeps my hair in place. I'm cold. I'm just wearing this for fun."

"Fun my ass. You look like a bum."

Sharkey fumbling in his shirt pocket for a piece of paper. Grabbing a pencil stub from the bar, writing down his son's name. "I want you to give this to the sergeant at arms so he can introduce you."

"No. The hell with it. I'm just an observer. Who's the sergeant at arms?"

"That guy standin' over there. Drum."

"Drum?"

"Drum. That's him."

"What about the guy next to me?"

"Well, I want to introduce you to everyone. That there's Paddy. Paddy, this here is Chuckie, my boy from Vietnam."

"Pleased to meet you, Chuckie," says Paddy. "The Legion needs more good men like your father here."

"That's for goddamn sure," says Sharkey.

Chuckie motioning to Taylor for another round of beer, turning his back to Sharkey for the moment, eager to talk with Paddy, to pick up the singsong in his voice, so reminiscent of his fire-team buddy in 'Nam, old Dinger Doyle.

AN AMERICAN PRESENCE

"You live around here?" he asks Paddy.

"Oh, no. I'm a block or so from the good mayor over in Bridgeport."

Chuckie turns to bring the old man into the conversation but spots him stepping into the john.

"Ah, he's a pearl of a man, Sharkey," says Paddy. "I've dealt with a number of service officers in my day, and there's not a one that comes even close to your father. Give the lad another beer, bartender."

Sharkey returning, hands thumping him on the back all the way to the bar.

"What's a service officer?" Chuckie asks the old man.

"You're lookin' at the poor bastard right-here. I take care of the men. I make out their claims for disability, compensation, pensions, crap like that. Right, Paddy? I answer their questions. I help people out. Ask any one of these guys what Sharkey does. My office is appointed, and I been at it for 25 goddamn years!

"A guy comes to me and he wants to go to the hospital, I help to get him in. A poor widow ain't got no money, I get her some money. We're a service organization. When you goddamn guys gonna understand that! We help people, that's all!

"Ask Paddy. He got banged up in the war, his compensation run out, not another service officer in the whole damn city could do diddly for him. He came to this post, I made a claim for him, and now he's gettin' his ten-percent compensation. Ain't that right, Paddy?"

"Absolutely. This man is interested in the truth. That's important. There isn't another man anywhere that will go after the truth as Sharkey does."

"You bet your ass!"

"Who's going to stick up for the vet?" asks Paddy. "Why, the government spends billions of dollars sending men into space and completely forgets about the vets, the fellas down here who fought to keep this country free."

"Yes, sir. Hey, Drum! My son, Chuckie. Viet vet. I want you to introduce him at the meetin'."

Sharkey handing Drum the piece of paper while telling his son, "You sit next to me over there. I'll let you know what the hell's going on."

Eight-thirty, Chuckie checking his watch. Focusing on the scene. Sharkey disappearing to relieve himself once again. Fourteen men present, Paddy pontificating on the youth of America.

"They're not a bad lot, most of them. There's much good in them I'm sure. What the government ought to do is start up the CCC camps again. That was a fine thing. The earth's important, you know. Erosion is a terrible thing. The youth ought to be in there pitching, stopping all the terrible erosion that's going on. There's nothing more precious than life, you know. Nothing more important than to learn the art of living."

On the muddy trail, early that morning between Da Nang and Hue, the Lance Corporal, the unofficial American observer, discovering last night's patrol. Six men, including Doyle, in pieces. Their wangs cut off, stuffed into their ears.

The interrogation of three gooks that afternoon, possible North Vietnamese, possible VC, possible anybodies, stretched on the ground. They all look the same. Covering their necks and private parts

with talcum powder — to check the bleeding, they've been told. Waving the machete over them. Any answers? Any questions? The unofficial American observer on the spot. "They do it to us, we do it to them," the official refrain.

Which side are you on, boy?

The unofficial American observer fading into the meeting. Eight forty-five. The scattered group of legionnaires entering the tiny hall, taking up positions on the folding chairs. Two and three men seated on three sides behind wooden pedestals, each draped with a blue-and-gold cloth: Justice, Loyalty, Democracy.

The Commander, James Sullivan, facing the gathering of legionnaires from a platform resembling a stage, a sanctuary. The men making an effort to stand at attention as the colors are posted.

The Lance Corporal, the unofficial American observer, the guest, waiting at the bar for Sharkey to return as the men of the Legion work out a quiet among themselves. The Assistant Adjutant reading a prayer. The door to the john left open while the sound of Sharkey aiming a steady stream enters the stillness. Emerging, making his way past the bar, picking up Paddy and Chuckie. The two men following Sharkey to his pillar: Democracy.

Still standing, the men pushing onward in a mumbled recitation of the American Legion Preamble: "... to uphold and defend the Constitution of the United States ... to maintain law and order ... to foster and perpetuate a one hundred percent Americanism...." The memory of the men reinforced by the entire preamble printed on the front wall behind the Commander in letters large enough to be read from the back bar.

THE GHOST OF SANDBURG'S PHIZZOG

"... To inculcate a sense of individual obligation to the community, state, nation ... to make right the master of the night ... to consecrate and sanctify our comradeship by our devotion to mutual helpfulness...."

The Commander asking Drum to introduce the guests, if there are any. Drum reading from the crumpled piece of paper given to him by Sharkey. The Lance Corporal rising in place. One legionnaire clapping. Sharkey whistling with two fingers, then reaching for his bottle under his chair. Wondering just what the hell Vietnam looks like anyway. Wondering if the snow is still falling.

The reading of the minutes of the last meeting by the Adjutant. Nothing happened at the last meeting. There was a dance with a modest turnout. The bar cleared about $30. Some discussion of bills and membership.

"We got to keep our membership up, or else we lose a delegate to the national convention," says the Adjutant. They have close to 250 members. They're down about ten. The unofficial American observer making a head count: 1, 2, 3, 4, 5, 6, 7, 8, 9, 10, 11, 12, 13, 14.

pan slowly ...

Commander James Sullivan calling for other reports. There are no other reports. Silence. Nothing happened but the last meeting. The Commander searching the stillness in the hall.

Then the service officer, Stanley Korczak, Past Commander, rising, pushing the chair back with his foot, knocking over an empty bottle, leaning into his pedestal, Democracy, with both hands, steering it, then straightening his cap with a thrust of dumb

AN AMERICAN PRESENCE

fingers, reporting to the Commander on the people he's helped since the last meeting.

Sharkey reading from a list he keeps folded in his wallet. All the claims he's helped settle. All the legionnaires and their families whose lives he's helped to make just a little more comfortable.

"When a man dies in this post, we don't forget him," explains Sharkey. "He's not just shit. We help the widow who lives on and on all over the place. We had a widow and daughter arrangement ... we settled that with a pension. We've had another one of our recent members apply for a pension, and he got it! We got another claim coming up, and they got it downtown there yet, whatever the hell they're doin' with it. Then there's this little 95-pound woman with her sick husband, and the poor thing's got to lift him out of bed with a chain hoist, and we got him aid and attendants, and he'll do a little better now. We helped another widow with a grave monument and whatever goes with it. We want to help out some of the Vietnam vets with some education when they come here sometime. You'll never see them in jail or a goddamn thing. They'll be good people."

Sharkey sitting down to a small round of applause.

The unofficial American observer opening his eyes wide to stem the sudden tears. He tries to remember, in detail, every action of his from the time he got up in the morning. How his eyes opened, the way he swung his feet out of bed.

Focus on the next item on the agenda. An election. Nominations for trustee are open. Paddy rising: "I nominate Sharkey."

"I accept," says Sharkey. "And I move that nominations be closed."

Hoots and laughter. Some kidding about a railroad job. But a man in a wheelchair makes a motion for the unanimous election of Sharkey. It is approved.

"Any unfinished business?" asks the Commander.

Silence.

"New business?"

"Wait. I got some new business," says the Adjutant. "We've decided there would be an olive-branch night, Friday night. So set your sights for a big party and a big night. Then the winter carnival's coming up. I bought a lot of good prizes. I need more help...."

cut to ...

An old WWI vet rising from his chair, saluting the stage, explaining to no one in particular that he's leaving because he has to get the car home by 9:30. He walks out, leaving the door open behind him.

The new business is completed, followed by a small hurrah to "Pass the golden pot!"

One of the legionnaires making the rounds with a small wooden barrel painted gold, urging everyone to contribute his loose change for a chance to win the raffle.

And following the man with the golden pot, another man with a wooden bowl. "For all the old people who can't afford to pay their dues and stuff," explains Sharkey.

final fanfare ...

Drum walking to the center of the floor with the golden pot. Sharkey pushing his long-haired son in the red bandanna and old fatigue jacket out front to draw the lucky number.

Chuckie pulling out 0016 and Drum relaying the

AN AMERICAN PRESENCE

number to the Adjutant sitting on the stage. The Adjutant explaining that he can't hear the number. Drum repeating it. The Adjutant searching his roster and coming up with the name: "Bluer? Blumer?"

"That's Bob Bloomer!" shouts Sharkey. "That son of a bitch never comes to meetings either."

The $7.38 stays in the pot. "There's as much as $35 in there sometimes," Paddy whispers to Chuckie.

The Assistant Adjutant closing with a prayer. The colors retired at 9:15. Red, white, and blue passing beside the unofficial American observer. One corner grazing his cheek. Feeling chilled, though he can't explain it. He's dressed. He's healed. He was never really hurt.

Once, in the heat of the battle for Hue City, the fight for the Citadel. Dying Delta, all of his company but him and ten men wiped out. Waiting, wanting to die. Then through the corner of a broken window frame the sight of someone lowering the North Vietnamese flag, raising the stars and stripes. Perspiration trickling down his forehead. Eyes burning and running. Witness to a whole battle turned around in an instant. A cold feeling of such a freedom to fire now at anything for the flag! He emptied himself of everything he had while old movies unreeled away within him, whatever remained to imagine.

The unofficial American observer sitting back at the bar with Paddy and Sharkey. Studies in patriotism. The immovable forces. In 'Nam they called it the American presence.

Paddy points to a sign at the far end of the bar.

THE GHOST OF SANDBURG'S PHIZZOG

"How do you like it?" he asks. The sign is a clock that says: NO DRINKING BEFORE 5. The face of the clock is all fives. Chuckie suddenly finding such humor uncontrollably funny.

Sharkey introduces his son to the effeminate Assistant Adjutant, Vince Stabille, who stares at the Lance Corporal intensely and finally nods and walks away. Only to return moments later and whisper in the Lance Corporal's ear: "I hate hippies who pose in old fatigue jackets."

At a table in one corner of the bar, two WWI vets and the Adjutant sit down to a game of poker and pass around a booklet of Irish sweepstakes tickets. Someone begins playing *The Tennessee Waltz* on the juke box in the hall. The Commander joins a few of his men at the other end of the bar for a drink.

Sharkey is angry because informed sources have told him that the Commander is angry with the way Sharkey handled the election of himself for trustee. What if there were real guests? asks the Commander. What if the Viet vets had showed? How would that have looked?

Sharkey doesn't give a damn what the Commander thinks.

Paddy is telling Chuckie about Sicily again, how he got hit, how he is forever thankful to Sharkey for getting him his ten percent disability compensation, $26 a month, and how he must still go in for a checkup once every month. He's telling him how, even now, in the middle of the night: "Should there be a backfire from a car's exhaust, I'll jump up in my bed and see me and my buddies in the field."

"There are only seven trustees," says Sharkey. "And when I get in there, there'll be only one hojo tellin' what to do. Me!"

AN AMERICAN PRESENCE

"It's a gentle post," confesses Paddy. "They don't hurt anything."

"This used to be a big post!" Sharkey suddenly hollering into Chuckie's face. "Then a group of them withdrew and formed their own post because they didn't like the beer drinkers here. That's what they thought of us — drunks. They formed their own post because they thought they were better than us — professionals. White-collar workers, dentists ... better than who, huh?"

Seaman Stanley Korczak, a WWII story in himself. The deck of the *Maryland* on fire. The *Nevada* on fire. The *Oklahoma* belly up. The *Arizona* sinking fast. Seaman Korczak jumping from the hellish deck, swimming under and through a flaming sea of oil and gas. Snatching men from the boiling waters. A hero born in fire.

"And what was it like for you, son?" Paddy tapping Chuckie on the shoulder.

Chuckie gently shaking him off. "I'm a blind, a window-and-shade man now," he smiles.

"Well, you did your duty."

"And he killed his share of gooks," says Sharkey, stumbling off to the john once again.

Commander Sullivan preparing to leave, taking Chuckie aside, inviting him to return. Chuckie finding himself apologizing for the poor turnout, the absence of Viet vets. The Commander shrugging his shoulders.

"What's going to happen?" he asks the Commander.

"Oh, we'll die, I guess. We got about ten years if we're lucky. The fellas from Vietnam don't want any part of it. It's a different time." Chuckie saluting him a gesture of goodbye.

THE GHOST OF SANDBURG'S PHIZZOG

"I was commander two years in a row," Sharkey barges in as Commander Sullivan turns and drifts toward the door. "Screw him. Nobody else wanted the job. 'Then I'll take the goddamn job again,' I said. The hell with these deadbeats. Taylor, a little firewater on ice."

The sound of Taylor smashing ice in the stainless-steel basin, dripping and clinking cubes into a glass, covering it over smoothly with whiskey while Sharkey and Paddy watch and Chuckie listens.

The Lance Corporal trying to put together words of a poem lost somewhere in high school. *Some say the world will end in fire ... Some say ice....*

"He won't tell you nothin', this kid," says Sharkey. "He won't tell you how many gooks he killed, he won't say diddly. I know, but I know! I got people downtown who can do things for me. I can find out your whole goddamn service record, 'cause I'm the service officer, you know, huh?" Sharkey laughing, taking hold of his son in his arm like a small kid wrapped in his father's forgiveness. Drinking to it. Rattling an empty glass of ice cubes in his hand.

We were going to have a party, Chuckie pictures it. It was July 4, 1968. Some of the guys had stolen some beer and some booze. There was a little ice plant in a village outside of Pu Bai. We bought two blocks of ice from the old man. He charged us $20.

When we got back to camp, we put the ice in vat cans and began chopping it for drinks. I poured two drinks of bourbon and ice. When I pulled my hands out of the chopped ice the third time, the vats were filled with blood. I never felt anything. Neither did the two guys who chugalugged the booze. The ice was filled with ground glass.

AN AMERICAN PRESENCE

When we got back to the ice plant, the old man was gone. But some of the villagers were still there. Men, women, children, and three babies were packed into the ice house. One crack shot from an M-16 from the back of a moving Jeep ignited a tank of gasoline alongside the building.

"Why the hell doesn't somebody say somethin'?" mumbles Sharkey. Taylor and Paddy putting on their coats, nodding goodbyes, disappearing into the dark hall. The door opening and closing.

fade in . . .

Sharkey fumbling for his keys outside the doorway, dropping his cap. Chuckie fixing it firmly on Sharkie's head. The two of them standing still in a snowy night of both darkness and light till Sharkey finally clicks the lock of the Legion hall in place.

Sharkey feeling for the ice in each step. Salt will take care of it for sure. The streets will be safe by morning.

dissolve . . .

The unofficial American observer following dark footprints which seem to widen and disappear behind him.

freeze . . . in a cold blue frame.

Ice it.

The Ghost of Sandburg's Phizzog

> *Now of course there are two Sandburgs ...*
> — Borges

Sandburg rising, a prairie, a harvest of wheat to his hair, spewing out a dry weed stuck between his teeth ... rubbing prairie rose from his eyes. Brushing both hands through his hair for that part, slightly to the right, combing each side down straight through his fingertips over the top of his ears.

Yawning, breaking, shoveling for his black shoes, his gray stockings. Baggy brown pants, wrap-around-twice worn leather belt, white shirt tucking-in back, sides, front. Galluses over the boney shoulders. Buttons. And a bow tie: blue.

Naw, I'll wear me a red bandanna today, gargling, sandpaper throat, bricklayer's hands ... parting the clean curtains, checking his phizzog in the glass. That face he's got. Ah, the looking-glass man ...

Time? The storyteller you can't shut up, he goes on.

Halsted Street, Harrison Street, Peoria Street ... the traffic in his eyes. Broken faces, police whistles, iron fences, loving hunger, Grant on his bronze horse in Lincoln Park under snow, a man singing, streetcars, neighbors at work, washerwoman, fish crier, cripples, passers-by with silence written on mouths, killers, working girls, masses of asses in the fog.

We were the people, maybe.

Sandburg shaking it off ... I wish to God I never knew you now.

Shaking off his phizzog, scattering myth in a puff of milkweed seed. Now cornhusker, haystack hair, cornflower eyes, golden squash skin, prairie wind stealing his songful breath.

THE GHOST OF SANDBURG'S PHIZZOG

I am, I am, I am ... dust, laughter, stars, radishes, eggs, frost, crow, kiss, water, muskrat, nigger, pumpkin, river, railway, limestone, walnut, potato blossom, concertina, melon, eagle, loam, lover ...

The ghost of Sandburg shoveling off to the streets, trailing a busted walnut guitar behind him. A bucket of mud, a pail of smoke, a pocket of Illinois prairie. No more.
I wish to God I never ...
Stockyard slaughtered, hogbutcher heaven, skyscraper stillborn.
They tell me you are crooked, are wicked, are brutal ... Yes, the people? The family of man? *Always the mob.*
Perish the people.
People putting handles on all the languages. Talk is cheap. Naming's become numbering. Hold. Still.
Shovel it all under, let me work.
I *was* the people, wasn't I? Chicago citizen, Illinois boy, Midwest meanderer.
Oh, I had a zoo inside me once ...

There is a baboon in me ...
I study the language of taverned souls, an intoxication still ...
"The old lady left. I threw her out. Women go crazy in their change-of-life. She was drinking a bottle of VO a day. Tomorrow I go to traffic court. I left her the car, you see, and she's been gettin all these goddam traffic tickets. All parking tickets mostly. She didn't think I'd know. But I got a letter to appear in court the other day for all those goddam traffic tickets she's been gettin. Well, they're in for a big

THE GHOST OF SANDBURG'S PHIZZOG

surprise if they think I'm goin to pay them. I'm just gonna tell them she left me, and she's got the car, and those tickets are all hers. What the hell can they do to me? If I get a nice judge, he'll understand. A good judge should understand about women. Hell, why should I have to pay for her mistakes?

"Three things happen to a woman when she goes through this. Either she hits the bottle for good, or she starts jazzin anything that moves, or she wises up. I know where she hangs out. Her friends tell me what she's doin. I know what she's doin every night. Drinkin like a fish, jazzin like a mink. Not wisein up at all.

"I'm workin on a trap. I got this dolly all lined up. Just me and this babe somewhere, and then my wife all of a sudden comin in and catchin us.

"If that don't work, then I'll divorce her. That's all. That's all I can do."

Everybody loved Chick Lorimer ... Nobody knows where she's gone ...

Let us be honest about women ... Ziegfeld girl, harlot, Mom, loving one easy, loving another hard ... I loved only one ... women of lights and nights and shadows, o beauty of no takers ... old woman asleep in the hallway, woman with her head flung between her knees, gypsy gal, the mouths of women, river lady, girl with a rose in her hair, lady with a laugh ... I know the birth of all your songs.

Mammy.

Sorrow shaken from white shoulders.

I wish to God, I wish to God, I wish to God ...

THE GHOST OF SANDBURG'S PHIZZOG

There is an eagle in me ...
   The ghost of Sandburg sups. Nighthawk hopper. Shadow and light.
   I have such a heart's hunger for you all ...
   "Yeah, but since I left Weight Watchers I'm on my own diet now, and I lost fifteen pounds all on my own. I eat everything. Almost everything. And I got a new pant suit, size eighteen, you should see me in it! I should wear it all the time. It's blue and it looks so nice on me. I'm happy in it. I could never wear anything like it before with my wide ass. Tonight I'm going dancing with my friend. He fixes watches. Yeah, so I gave him this watch to fix. I'm always breaking watches. You're supposed to shake them like this when they stop. When my husband was alive, he'd fix them like this, you know ... bang the hell out of them on the table. And so I do the same thing. But my friend who fixes watches says you're not supposed to do that with watches. He taught me how to handle them. You're supposed to just shake them gently like this. But I can't. I still bang the hell out of them, and they still don't work. Naw, it's nothing serious. He's just a friend. He's a nice guy. We go to a lotta places together. We have a good time. No motels or nothing. We can go to my place for that if we want. Why spend money on a motel? How do you like this watch? It's hot. I spent five bucks on it. My watch-fixer thinks it's worth twenty-five bucks. He's different. I never went nowhere with my husband. He liked to just stay around the house. That was all right. And then he died. He was a policeman. We buried him in his uniform. It was real nice. He had his stamps and his coins ... he had his own things to do. And when he was going to the

THE GHOST OF SANDBURG'S PHIZZOG

hospital, the last thing he said was, 'Toodle loo.' He thought he was coming back, you know. And when they told me, I just screamed. That's all. But I kind of think he knew he was going, you know? The last few months he kept asking me about his policies. One of the kids wanted to cash in a policy for a car. And he kept asking me where that policy was for the kid. We don't have it, I told him. We have three twenty-year endowment policies, that's all. Three of them. And he was painting and fixing things around the house. He knew he was going to go. He made me an end table out of bricks. I always wanted an end table out of bricks and he never made me one. Make me an end table out of bricks, I'd tell him. I'm gonna make you an end table out of bricks now, he said, just before he went. And he did. It was so nice. I painted it white and decorated it with ivy and everything. It's funny how he was doing all these things like he wasn't gonna be around. My oldest kid is a missionary in Indochina. He was in Indochina all last year and this year he's coming home. Next year he's going back to Indochina. Last week me and my friend went to New Salem. I want to know all about Lincoln. Tomorrow me and my friend are going to the museum. I never knew so much was inside museums before. I want to find out about the laser beam. My kid knows all about it so I want to learn something about laser beams so I know what he's yaking about when I see him. Last year I went to the Planetarium around Christmas to see the star of the East. It's supposed to be in the same place it was when Christ was born. But I couldn't find it. Jesus, my car is really a wreck. Yesterday the muffler fell off, and the goddam thing was just hanging there.

THE GHOST OF SANDBURG'S PHIZZOG

What am I gonna do? I yelled in the middle of the street. And then some kid on a bike came by and tied it up with his patrol belt. With his patrol belt! Jesus, I tell you I've been having more fun. I never went anywhere before, now I go everywhere. Tonight I'm going dancing. Do you know the new dances? There's nothing to them. You just keep moving. We never knew when it'll be us, you know. We've all got to face the same battle. I like to move fast."

Neighborhood. Backyards, fences, gangways, alleys, street lamps, garbage cans, milk wagons, ice wagons, junk wagons ... "Raaaaaaggg-saaaaa-Lionnnnn," kick-the-can, cherry trees, robins, apple trees, sparrows, elms, Lombardy, catalpas with long thin black cigars for smoking, morning glories, gutters, wooden steps, front porches, back porches, Hide-and-Seek, "Here I come ready or not!" corner taverns, buckets of beer, pinochle, priest, parish, "Step on a crack and break your mother's back," woodsmoke, burning leaves, squirrel, robin, bluejay, screens, moths, crystal sets, radio, the polka hour, concertina, dumplings, sauerkraut, workingstiffs, homemade wine in the basement ...

A light in the basement window ... the ghost of old man Daruva turning the spigot on a fifty gallon barrel of homemade Yugoslav wine, filling a mason jar, slumping on a stool near the cement basin, feeling the presence of the past.

Daruva, slaughtering stockyard Slav, blood shoveler ... the ghost of Sandburg sipping wine beside him, the work and the weary, taking up a song:

I dreamed I saw Joe Hill last night
Alive as you and me

THE GHOST OF SANDBURG'S PHIZZOG

"Why Joe, you're ten years dead," I said.
"I never died," says he.
Daruva squeezing the wine of the mason jar tight in both hands, steeped in blood ... No vork, no money, vork, no money, is no good, nothing. Is same! Is always altogether same ...
I knew that the WPA
Can't do a thing for me.
Daruva, a broken jar of wine at his feet, the stool upturned, dangling by a lampcord like a side of beef from the basement rafters.
"I never died," says he.

There is a fox in me ...
    I stand before the place that was once Minsky's
        burlesque.
    I hang around a while, hankering for the drum
        roll and the baggy pants comic, the
    screech of the curtain, the dancer with the moon
        in her hair.

**AND NOW STRAIGHT FROM PARIS JUST
    BACK FROM A SWING
THROUGH SOUTH AMERICA HERE
    NOW LIVE ON STAGE
STORMY!**

Oh, she was young, oh, she was blond, oh, she was
    beautiful, and oh, she could
dance a Lake Michigan moon out of the water and
    onto her hair.

Swaying in black velvet, she moved out of the river
    within me,
Oh, prairie night, oh, dark thunder, oh,
    shimmering woman, I am one of your boys.

THE GHOST OF SANDBURG'S PHIZZOG

For Stormy could bump and she could grind and
   she could bump
And she could grind, and she could promise you
   everything
Even up there in the last row of the highest
   balcony.

And she could bounce it to you and to you and to
   you
And you knew she could promise you everything
   and never deliver the goods.

Cause Stormy could bump and she could grind
   and she could put her hands
On her hips and guarantee all moveable parts
   cause Stormy vibrated the
Language of burlesque and had mastered the art of
   the bump and the grind
And the terrible taunting technique of the tease.

She bumped it to the boys in the first five rows,
She threw it to a mailman, ready to receive and
   deliver her message
In all kinds of weather.

Oh, she could bend and she could shake and she
   could throw her head
Right into your lap ... She could dance until the
   Broadway Limited left
The next day, and she could bump all night
   moving freight through silent
Fields of tall corn, with only a whistle for song.

She could strip to the essentials, moving it barely
   at all,
Cause Stormy stripped clean was anti-climatic,
   cause Stormy all in

THE GHOST OF SANDBURG'S PHIZZOG

Her finery was burlesque bonafide ...

... the boom-da-da-boomda-da-boom of the drums,
the drop of the gloves,
the swish of the hips,
the toss of the moonily hair,
the backside journey of a zipper,
the coyly turned head, and the wink,
the this-is-what-you've-been-waiting-for-boys,
as Stormy turns and bares to face all the world of Minsky's,
and the lights go out and the curtain and the curtain screeches shut,
and the music and the hand-clapping and the shouts,
and I tell you there was nothing in the world like this,
        but a wind died down.

The babbling tongues of the people, that was mine. I talked turkey. I loved tongue ... *I rise out of my depths with my language: gabby, plugged nickel, slambang, wigwag-ging, gazook, babbler, pig-sticker, Dago, baboon, Hunky, riffraff, humdrum, goofy, ooze, huggermugger, on the fritz, bunkshooter, Wop, cockeyed, skiddoo, the little two-legged joker, lickety-split, pal, ramshackle, ragtime jig, hoosegow, phooey, son-of-a-gun, coolie, snootful, dopey, wrongheaded fool, gimme mazuma* ...

You rise out of your depths with your language: persona, unreal, I don't believe it, beautiful, fantastic, super, too much, cool, bad, laid-back, doing, bottom line, viable, nuances, syndrome, uptight, real per-

THE GHOST OF SANDBURG'S PHIZZOG

son, doing your own thing, dynamite ...
    Dynamite super farout laid-back me, doing poetry ...
    Well, I'm doggone happy, a gabby mouth, my heart goes pit-a-pat; I'm just a polooka, young feller, loony lingo, a broken face gargoyle, a jabberer with a snootful of plain words, horsefeathers, rubbernecks, no baloney ... gimme Shee-caw-go, ragtag and bobtail, the rabble, the peepul!
    Where to? What next? There are no handles upon a language.

Lines based on certain regrets that come with rumination upon the painted faces of women on North Clark Street, Chicago
    Women of the night, dark side, shadow light, back streets of the black heart, painted women under the gas lamps luring the farm boys ... Businessmen, fathers, suburban church leaders, conventioneers, policemen, firemen, Billy-Grahamed beings, small town sheriffs, midnight poets all ... all beating a path to Salvation, Your name is Woman ... They tell me you are wicked, and I can't believe them ...
    COMPLETELY NUDE ... EXCITING YOUNG WOMEN ...
    MANICURES ... BODY PAINTING
"Hi," she says, leaning into the closed door.
Hello, I reply. I'm Carl Sandburg. You probably never heard of me before.
"Nope."
I've had such a longin for for a manicurin in this City of Big Shoulders.
"All right," she says without smiling. "I'll explain the rules."

THE GHOST OF SANDBURG'S PHIZZOG

Rules, Ma'm? I didn't come to play poker or write a sonnet.
"I undress completely, but there's no touching beneath the waist. Remember that.
Did you come for a manicure or a body painting, did you say?"
Well, I came to finally realize a painted woman ... but I do have this bad case of writer's cramp, stiff joints ...
"Okay. You've got fifteen minutes."
For what?
She smiles and proceeds to tell a poor poet what else a body can do with itself, if a body cared to, while she disrobes, dismantles ...
Did you ever hear of Minsky's?
She shakes her head, no.
I could maybe write a poem about you this way ... luring the farm boys, I think.
Cornstalk thin, dry, vulnerable, sad as a scarecrow.
Please, I can see all there is to see. Is this all a body's worth, fifteen bucks? Don't you even dance?
"Just a look and a manicure, Buster."
Exciting young woman, these are sensitive fingers, careful now.
"Are you a doctor?"
No, a gabber, a babbler, a wordsmith.
"What's that?"
Someone who goes around and just keeps talking to himself, hoping others will hear how carefully he speaks to them.
"You're not law and order, are you?"
That's a fine question. I play tennis without a net, so it's been said.
"Do you want to paint me?" she asks, holding a palette of colors.

THE GHOST OF SANDBURG'S PHIZZOG

He dips his fingers in green paint and writes the word "prairie" just beneath her navel. He blows it dry, then touches his lips to it.

"Once I was painted with birds," she says. "Once with flowers. And there was a guy who came in here one time, a minister, who knelt before me, then painted the ten commandments on me from my neck to my knees."

There are some things even a poet can't imagine in his own city. Some things that make no sense at all and are best kept in the dark, in that zoo inside ourselves.

"Are you through, Buster? Cause your time is up. God, what a phizzog you got."

There is a wolf in me ...

Sandburg, beseiged by contemporary bullshitters, dressed in saffron robes, dressed in white, dressed in black, on all the contemporary Chicago corners ... gimme mazuma or it's Hell's bell ... Sandburg hightailing it for west Madison, pausing briefly beneath Claes Oldenberg's Batcolumn, smiling ... *Here is a tall bold slugger* ... then skiddadling for a mission on Madison, still searching for *the* word.

He takes a back seat. His phizzog lost in a sorrowful sea of faces, brother, can you spare a dime, waiting to be fed ... but not just yet ... first, the Word to fill the stomach, stem the hunger pains.

The Reverend Cracker appears singing, "Something Got a Hold of Me Last Night," urging every last man Jack to stand, I SAID STAND! while he and his cronies pray out loud. Cracker ascends a high platform studying every face, including Sandburg's phizzog.

"How many you men had the flu?" he hollers. "Some people tell me Heaven's like Chicago!" he taunts. "SOME PEOPLE TELL ME HEAVEN'S LIKE SKID ROW," he screams.

One crony plays a guitar, another a violin. One begins to sing, "There's One Way, One Way to God," Cracker joining in. Sermon, song, sermon, song, sermon, song . . . the song of hungry stomachs.

Brother, I am fire . . . seethes Sandburg.

"Last Night I Dreamed an Angel Came," sings Cracker. A black man closes his eyes and sways gently with the song.

"Say 'Amen,'" says Cracker.

"Amen," say the men.

"THAT'S ALL YOU MEN ARE IS DIAMONDS IN THE ROUGH," screams Cracker. "THAT'S ALL. THAT'S ALL. AM I RIGHT, MEN? AM I RIGHT? HOW MANY YOU MEN THINK THE REVEREND CRACKER'S RIGHT? SEE? SEE? NOW ALL YOU MEN THERE SAY THE REVEREND CRACKER SPEAKS THE TRUTH, SAY IT! THERE . . . THERE . . . NOW ALL YOU MEN SAY, 'AMEN.'"

You come along squirting words at us, shaking your fist and calling us all damn fools so fierce the froth slobbers over your lips . . .

"HOW MANY YOU MEN THINK WE SHOULD THROW THAT MAN OUT? HOW MANY YOU MEN THINK HE SHOULD STAY BUT KEEP HIS MOUTH SHUT? . . . NOW ALL SAY, 'PRAISE BE THE LORD' . . . THAT'S RIGHT .. THAT'S GOOD . . . YOU KNOW, THAT'S THE MOST SENSIBLE THING YOU

THE GHOST OF SANDBURG'S PHIZZOG

SAID ALL DAY ... There's NOBODY deserves to hear the truth TWICE if they heard it ONCE!"
I like to watch a good four-flasher work ...

I will be the word of the people.
Mine will be the bleeding mouth
from which the gag is snatched.
I will say everything.

There is a fish in me ...
Midnight. Sandburg at the bar in the Billy Goat Tavern, listening to a young newspaperman ...
"I was out of it. I found that if I could just make it to work in the morning and back home at night, that would be an accomplishment. Just to get there and to get back. The rest of the day was a haze. I could not function. And if a man cannot function, a man is totally lost.

"I was hallucinating. I was paranoid. There was no me, nothing whatsoever. I tried a psychologist. Ha, he was something. A few weeks after I began going to him, he shot his own wife.

"I know what the depths are, believe me. I know what hell is all about. I was so psychotic I could have killed a man. I'm sure of that. I wouldn't have done it. No, no, no ... I wouldn't have killed a person. But I could have. And that's the frightening thing. I share every murderer's heart now. And that's the wonder, that we are brothers.

"I understand Hesse now, and all the business of being reborn. When you're down that far, some-

THE GHOST OF SANDBURG'S PHIZZOG

thing must happen. After my psychologist shot his wife I realized that no one, nobody was going to help me. If I was to survive, it would depend on me.

"So I began with just a few things, mundane tasks that I could accomplish. Like washing the windows, cutting the lawn. Little daily accomplishments. Gradually I built upon them. Physical things.

"Mind and body. That is really an important thing. I had let my body go to waste. I was fat, sloppy, ugly. So I began to work on this. Putting my body back in shape. That's why I took up diving. I discovered the significance of my body in the way my mind worked.

"I discovered all sorts of things about myself, about my life under water. Water is grace. Water is a way to live. It is such a fantastic world down there. I love to dive off the Keys in Florida. The clarity under water is so pure it is astounding. I can see for a half a mile or more.

"The fish swim right beside me. I've had a barracuda this long look right into my mask and turn, and swim right along with me. They are not startled. It is almost as if I am one of them. I love life under water."

And when has creative man not toiled deep in myth?

    Sandburg sunrise . . . doffing his cap to the ghost of Daley in the Civic Plaza . . . Sandburg bidding adieu, a Polaroid camera in hand, asking a city worker to take a shot of him under the Picasso.

    Click . . . Sandburg's smiling phizzog . . . the black pools of Picasso's eyes shining down upon him . . . the dimple on Daley's double chin, winking.

THE GHOST OF SANDBURG'S PHIZZOG

Sandburg merging with morning down Dearborn, melting into mosaic Chagall, seesawing through Calder's red stabile, snapping photos of a free floating poem.

Sauntering Sandburg on LaSalle Street, tossing wooden nickels into the doorways of all the bank buildings ... then rising to the heights of Sears Tower.

Sandburg quaffing a dark beer at Berghoff's ...

Sandburg haunting Kroch's & Brentano's in search of himself ...

Sandburg riding an Art Institute lion ...

Sandburg sitting at a table, nodding off, reading himself in the Chicago Public Library:

Let me be monosyllabic today, O Lord ...
   a crony of old men
   who wash sunlight in their fingers and
   enjoy slow-pacing clocks.

Sandburg on the bridge, Michigan and Wacker, perusing the Gothic heights of the *Chicago Tribune* building, laughing with his white teeth, turning to the *Chicago Sun-Times*, remembering the old *Daily News* ... under the terrible burden of destiny laughing as a young man laughs ... then boarding the Mercury Sightseeing Boat under the bridge for a last view from the lake, city of the floating shoulders, and a final winding farewell down the Chicago River, head singing so proud to be alive and coarse and strong and cunning ... the ghost of Sandburg ascending on cat feet, river trailing from his shoulders in fog, nocturne in a deserted urban landscape, the Sandburg spectre floating Chagall blue rivernight, starnight, moonlight, merging all the waterways ... Rock River, Fox River, Chicago River,

THE GHOST OF SANDBURG'S PHIZZOG

Desplaines River, Kankakee River, Illinois River ... downstate, O Sangamon, Kaskaskia, Little Wabash, Little Muddy ... O home in Illinois.

I find myself in prairie ... my peace, my past. I need prairie to pitch into, plant myself, dream myself corn, loam, wheat, grass, goldenrod, red rooster, yellow summer rain, oak, daisy, dark running water, farmer, flat land, horse, honey locust, purple thistle, crabapple, hollyhock, prairie rose, crow, meadow, dogwood, thrush, rock, violet, redbud, hawthorne, prairie woman, moss, barn, snow, owl, ice, seed, prairie man, blizzard, corncrib, wind, silo, chicken, dog, limestone, bushel basket, hazel nut, spade, goat, plow, Holstein cow, north star, bullfrog, graveyard, haystack, Abe Lincoln, prairie child ...
The story lags.
The story has no connections.
The story is nothing but a lot of banjo
 plinka plinka plunks.
Time? The storyteller you can't shut up ...

Son, you ain't seen nothin yet ...

I lean into a prairie wind, plant an acorn, be an acorn, become an oak, spreading my arms into branches, holding hawk, owl, crow, cradling them gently, lifting them off, I am trees I am woods I am forests, wind dancer, twilight, horizon, first star, deepest night, harvest moon, daybreak, the rising sun ...

rooster crow, robin song, dog bark, the splash of a frog, the whir of a windmill, the neigh of a horse, the hum of an insect, the banging of a screen door, the smell of coffee perking ...

I stretch and lie down in prairie grass, chuckle

over my own phizzog in blue heaven looking glass, slip a long thin green weed between my teeth, play with it gently inside my mouth ...

I extend my arms beside me beyond reach, working a pair of angel wings in earth as a child would do in snow, working my legs the same way ... Kickapoo, I say, Chillicothe, papoose, caboose, hallelujah on top a dung pile, bypaths, gravestones, bandannas and a wagonload of radishes ... plinka, planka, plunk, my guitar has strummed itself into bird ...

Working myself on the earth, into earth, till the image is shrouded in prairie, the earth angel becomes shadow, becomes light while grasses rise all around once more — two prairie roses for what the eyes once saw, and wind tickling the longest thin straw held in a mouthful of roots, jabbering in me still.

Dwelling

Lying in bed Jack hears the trap spring and jerks away from Hope beside him. His face feels cold; his eyes are teary. He recalls the heaving of his body in dream, the sound of someone sighing. He buries his fists in the sockets of his eyes and rubs the wetness away.

Blurry on the edge of sleep, Jack attempts to retrieve what awakened him this cold gray morning now taking shape in windows, a dresser, an oval mirror, and the blue blanketed body of Hope curled away from him. Closing his eyes, he seeks return, refuge in some passionate sorrow, undefined, leaving him bereft of grief and the warmth of tears upon awakening. Yet sensing it before in darkness. Shapeless. And loving its dumb life.

He hears the throbbing of his own blood and is aware that the sigh now coming from him changes to a moan, the same sound he made as a child to numb whatever pain inhabited his body. The moan would hum through his flesh, reverberate in his bones, his very teeth, stilling him, bringing his mother who would sit on the edge of the bed, a rosary still in hand, and rest her cool palm on his forehead, then test his temperature with her lips.

He watches the day move in closer over the back of Hope's shoulder, watches a branch stir as the silhouette of a small bird edges along it till the end dips by the weight and the bird scatters into flight. He hears the cry of a gull over the rooftop, a fishing tug chugging through the strait of Port des Morts. The bottom of Hope's feet are cold as they brush against his bare legs and spring away.

He turns himself tightly into the edge of the blanket away from Hope. Everything is burrowing in.

THE GHOST OF SANDBURG'S PHIZZOG

Fox, coons, skunk, burrowing in. Mice returning to the house from their weedy tunnels in the fields. Hope hears mice in her sleep, sees them. They are nesting in her dresser drawers again, she tells Jack. They are storing seeds in the pockets of her fashionable coats she no longer wears since moving to the country. She is certain the mice find their way from the cellar.

Set the traps, Jack, before you go to bed, she says. Upstairs and downstairs.

The snap of the spring sometimes awakes him at night, a witness to struggle, to death, while Hope whispers vacantly in her sleep: Did you set the traps, Jack?

He tries to recall this morning, or some time ago, suffering a thin cry from a sprung trap, and is uncertain now whether it came from the mouth of the tiny creature or his own.

Jack gets out of bed, puts on his clothes hanging from the doorknob, opens the closet, and carries the dead mouse to the downstairs porch where he discovers the other trap overturned. Nudging it with his foot, he is surprised by the color and shape of the creature. Not the usual brown and white field mouse, but a charcoal gray colored mole.

Why should he be startled? But he is. Opening the closet makes him anxious. What will he find this time? What's waiting for him? A closet floor covered with trapped mice? A snake? Once, on Hope's insistence, he left a trap set outside the cellar steps only to find a dead wren the next morning. See? See? He tossed the trap with the wren in the field.

He lifts the spring, shakes the mouse and the mole free in the same field, and puts the empty traps in the

DWELLING

pockets of his old jacket. Already the mouse and mole have disappeared from sight. He imagines the elements or animals will take care of the remains. It is a blind gesture of no consequence. In all his walks through the field, spring, summer, and fall, he has never come upon the remains of any of the mice or even the trapped wren. Memory abandoned. Guilt or death somehow assuaged. Nature absolves the unliving and leaves no evidence of life. While the machinery of death, its fear and celebration, rests in the minds and hands of men.

He imagines birds dying in flight, dropping from the sky and disappearing. The anonymity of insects. He sees himself on a walk one day, dropping in his tracks and that ending it. But for Hope, who would find him and mourn his passing. His soul would never rest.

Moving to the country makes him think these things, more than he wants to. More than he is supposed to, since the doctors advised a change of scene would do him good, clear his mind of the confusions of city life. The plots within the agency in Chicago to weaken his influence. The burden and desire of other women. The sudden loss of a parent. The fear of violence — escaping with his life twice —though some, including Hope, deign it simple paranoia. Though suffering in his mind, is never simple.

What works best is the silence. Some of the yoga he learned with the group in the hospital. Sitting still here in the fields, in proper position. Though he sees there is no silence. Everything becomes louder when you determine to no longer listen. It swallows you.

Nature seems to him a deep hole where things might willfully be abandoned or unexpectedly

THE GHOST OF SANDBURG'S PHIZZOG

emerge. He thinks of the town dump, now closed by the state environmental board. The huge pit covered with earth, returned to plant and animal life. And in spite of No Trespassing signs, people continue to appear at night with lanterns and shovels and large plastic bags, burying and unearthing things.

For breakfast he has a slice of toast, a glass of apple cider, and coffee. He moves with stealth around the kitchen, careful not to make any noise which might awaken Hope. Opening the refrigerator door, removing a spoon from the drawer of utensils, the sudden perking of the coffeepot, might easily betray him. For Hope to come down the stairs and join him for breakfast would make his day irretrievable.

What she does is magnify the moment, beginning with simple objects. This coffee mug for instance. Why doesn't he take a clean one? Would he please pour her a cup while he is at it. And make some orange juice or cut a grapefruit. Is there enough milk for supper? Maybe he should go into town today and buy another gallon. Did he catch any mice? She heard them all night in the walls. Someone told her they should stuff steel wool around the holes of the plumbing and heating pipes in the floor, leading up from the cellar. Mice get in that way. Would he do that, Jack?

He drinks his coffee standing, staring out the window toward the road, the field, the garden. Moments later he will find himself within the very scene he contemplates. A fragment of last night's dream about a wet iron fence comes to him, and then he loses it. Goldenrod, milkweed, and wild aster occupy the fields. The summer birds have thinned, their song diminished by cries of gulls and ravens. A

DWELLING

time between times, neither summer nor fall. A season of ambivalence which unsettles a man.

He is neither young nor old. Semi-retired, in Hope's words, from a Chicago ad agency for which he might still freelance, though he can no longer relate to his once-sophisticated campaigns of city men and city women on the prowl, images of desire — cologne, clothing, alcoholic beverages. Jack himself, as he was. One can appeal to almost any need in man, capture that desire, convince him his life can be different. For a while.

But there is no solid footing in any of it. Either in building false images of a new self through commerce, creating them in a swaying high-rise 45 stories above a city, or trying to maintain a life 33 floors above lawless streets with security personnel guarding your every entrance and exit.

He is a man on the mend in the rural midwest whose mind still plays tricks on him. Sometimes he begins to dial long distance, forgetting the name of the party. Sometimes, upon awakening, he stands beside the bed staring at the body he has left behind buried beneath the covers. Hope?

The woman he has been married to for more than twenty years. The mother of one daughter in college in Washington. The nurse who counts his pills each day and controls his moods.

Who is this woman with the salt and pepper hair in my bed? Who has abandoned whom? Why has love been reduced to caretaking? Why does he feel nothing except in dreams which he cannot remember?

He is surprised to find himself alone in a field when he is certain he is standing on a downtown cor-

THE GHOST OF SANDBURG'S PHIZZOG

ner in Chicago in spring, a young woman on his arm, waiting for the light to turn green. A flock of gulls wheels and keens in the wake of a farmer on his tractor turning over the earth in a far field. Preparing for winter, preparing for spring.

In the bedroom Hope ties a robe around herself and pounds the window shut with her fist. The wood is warped. She is cold and her hand now burns. The paint is flaking on the sill. The screen is rusted through. Nothing gets fixed.

The roof needs repair. Water is seeping into the house above the living room windows, leaving ugly stains on the wall. Despite the falling temperatures, the furnace failed to go on again last night. There was no sound of hot water gurgling through the pipes. Or she would have heard. Only mice scurrying in the walls. Jack will have to set some traps.

Pouring herself a cup of coffee at the table downstairs, Hope is drawn to the small crack in the corner of the kitchen window. She reaches toward it and runs her finger over the sharp edge, pushing it back evenly in place, cutting the skin cleanly. No pain or blood, just a mild stinging sensation. The garden must be picked and covered tonight or everything will freeze.

Jack notices in the garden that only the higher leaves of the pumpkin plants were caught by the first frost last night. It is time to cover the tomatoes, to put old bedspreads over the green peppers and cucumbers. Hope will pick the remainder of the wax beans, slightly boil and freeze them so they will be fresh tasting when served all winter.

Hope presses the cut finger between her lips, then stands staring through the cracked glass, catching a

DWELLING

distortion of Jack bending in the garden. There are two of him. Turning her head slightly this way and that way, she observes his body lengthen, turn serpentine, shrink, disappear. And now there he is again, just like normal. She leaves him so, bending in the garden, and walks into the living room, turning the thermostat up and down twice. The furnace fails to fire.

Jack! she calls out the back porch door.

Jack pinches a dead leaf from the hollow stem of a winter squash and pierces his thumb with a thorn so soft and imperceptible he cannot locate the pain. He feels it momentarily and then it is gone. He cannot find where the thorn went in. But somewhere in his body he knows there is a pain that may come and go for days like a thin sliver of wood which gradually works itself into the system, softens and disappears.

The sharp iron fence of an old cemetery. A spear pierces the hand of the boy climbing over. The language on the heart-shaped stone is all foreign.

Jack! The furnace won't go on!

She closes the door and lights the kitchen oven to take the chill out of the morning air. She brushes crumbs from the table into her hand and brushes them again into the waste basket. He pretends he doesn't hear me, she says.

There is a noticeable absence of the human voice in the country. Occasionally, depending on the wind or density of fog, the presence of mist, Jack hears a man in some distant farmyard but is unable to make any meaning of what he is saying. He imagines the man is alone, talking to horses or cows, for no one else can be heard. Only animal sounds. The sound of a solitary human voice suspended in mist comforts

THE GHOST OF SANDBURG'S PHIZZOG

Jack in the way he once knew and loved women who were strangers to his daily life.

The tomatoes are still green on the vine, he notices, walking between the rows. It is too far north, too short a growing season for them to ripen in time. Some could be salvaged, picked green, wrapped in newspapers and stored on the back porch. Each spring brought the threat of a late frost, while an early frost in fall could kill an entire garden in mid-August. All life seemed poised now in precariousness. Men at night had begun to shine deer from the road, holding their golden eyes in the beams of power lights, divining the herd's movement in fields and woods, catching their stillness in place, hoping for a November kill.

Turning over a row of old lettuce with a spade, Jack drives the point of it hard into the earth with a one-handed thrust and walks into an adjoining field to follow a shadowy movement through the weeds. Holes of burrowing animals are scattered everywhere. An opening in a patch of milkweed attracts his attention. And just a few feet from it, another burrow, freshly dug, with earth and pebbles strewn in piles about the entrance. He sits without moving a long time, expecting to see whatever went in, come out. Hearing a door close and the sound of Hope's voice down the road, he lies flat on his stomach, a hand hanging in each hole.

Jack?

He turns his head slightly to catch just a profile of her tugging cornstalks with both hands, tossing them on a pile resembling a grave. The garden is Hope's domain, planting, cultivating, weeding, thinning the rows of vegetables, picking food for the

DWELLING

table. She loves the earth for its physical demands and feels rewarded for her efforts.

Jack? Can you hear me?

Resting a cheek against the weeds, he hears his heart, feels a warmth generating through his body. He opens and closes his hands in the burrows, extends his fingers, reaches, and slowly pulls himself deeper. The earth is warm and moist at arm's length. He pauses there, envisioning a snarling mouth, teeth, a rabid wound.

He sees the earth beneath as passive, fecund, a dark passageway. A small child in his father's yard, digging a hole to China. A grown man remembering an American Indian myth of creation, an opening in the earth, First Man, First Woman, the Holy People emerge. He reaches as far as he is able, wanting to touch, to clear the way.

Jack!

His knees rest comfortably in natural hollows. His torso nestles in the weeds. He is settled. He holds the earth inside him. He lifts his mother, raising her higher in the hospital bed. He rolls a woman on top of him, kisses her, and buries his head, in sleep, in the back of Hope gathered in his arms. He holds the earth beyond reach, inching ahead, till his two hands unexpectedly meet, and he holds himself there, caught in his own foolishness.

Jack! The furnace. It won't go on. Do you hear me? Check the furnace.

He waits till he sees her bending in the garden again, her back to him, before he rises and drifts quickly toward the back field, the edge of the woods, out of her range of vision. He unhooks the cellar door and crouches toward the furnace.

THE GHOST OF SANDBURG'S PHIZZOG

The furnace, a concession to Hope, has ruined his root cellar, his wine cellar, and destroyed all the attraction an old farm cellar once held for him with its aroma of apples, onions, potatoes, cabbage, and fresh earth. Shelves of peaches, pears, pickles, tomatoes, preserved in blue and clear Mason jars.

There were no cellars in his boyhood, only basements of concrete floors, cement wash basins, coal furnaces, hot water heaters, and workbenches with steel vises where men of the house worked with tools and made repairs. Though a vague childhood memory remained, an image of his grandmother's basement, cellar-like with foods and smells, where harsh sounds of the old tongue could be heard, where people of the same blood gathered, where the family once dwelled.

With the installation of a central heating system, the heat was more evenly distributed, and Hope no longer froze in the upstairs bedroom nor spent her winters huddled over space heaters in the kitchen and living room.

Yet all the deterioration of the house in the past few years, from the leaky roof to the smell of decay in its structure, Jack attributes to the new heating system.

First the apples began to rot in the cellar, then the bushels of potatoes, cabbages, squash, and the large onions that hung in braids from the rafters. The wine turned bitter. The natural, earth-cooled temperature of the cellar year round was now warmed by the furnace from early fall to late spring. Everything smelled of oil and was covered with a fine coat of soot.

The solution was a root cellar behind the house which Jack began digging that first spring after the

DWELLING

furnace was installed, but which he finally abandoned in desperation. There were too many rocks and layers of limestone for him to dig by hand. The geology of the area was such that good earth seldom amounted to more than a matter of inches. Farmers pulled stone boats through the fields each spring. Jack was always digging rocks out of the garden for Hope. The oldtimers spoke of dynamiting cellars in the past, but that had been prohibited or strictly regulated in the recent rural revival as more city people began buying the land in small parcels of an acre or two, called mini-farms, and the state environmental board feared the possible contamination of water in old and new wells.

The few apples and garden produce Hope tried to store she kept in burlap bags and bushel baskets on the back porch where eventually gnawing mice or freezing temperatures ruined them. Each year a good portion of the harvest slowly decayed and was returned to the garden as compost. This was no loss in Hope's mind, merely an investment, a fair exchange. Jack could be seen on the newly plowed road in winter, a bushel of rotting fruit and vegetables at his feet, lobbing potatoes and apples in the snow covered garden like a kid tossing baseballs to the outfield, only watching them disappear into perfectly round holes of their own making.

The more even displacement of heat in the house caused the windows to fog at times, making it difficult for Jack to watch winter birds at the feeders or experience the restfulness of falling snow. When the temperature dropped below zero, all the panes turned opaque, illumined in blue-white fronds of frost. A jungle, in Jack's eyes, African, South

THE GHOST OF SANDBURG'S PHIZZOG

American. He would lose himself there in the glass. While Hope blew and rubbed a clear circle to see the outside.

It was a moisture problem, said the heating man. The roof began to leak because the ice which had always formed in winter along the roof's edge now began to melt as the heat from the new registers along the inside wall rose straight up. During the night, as temperatures dropped, ice formed again on the roof. While during the day, in the sun's heat, some of the ice melted into pools of water which eventually backed up under the shingles, slowly working its way through the roof boards and down the inside walls, leaving stains which Hope continually covered with paint each spring, only to watch them reappear in a matter of weeks. The house felt damp. The entire inner structure now harbored a moisture condition leading to decay. Hope wanted to rebuild the house, inside and out. Or burn the place down to the ground and begin anew. A smaller place. All on one level. Just a concrete slab, no cellar or basement. Well insulated. Tight.

Jack could hear the house breathe on windy days. He could follow the sagging roofline from the road and take pleasure in a place coming to rest. The house was settling, amiably, perfectly, as many of the white-frame farmhouses nearby, in need of a coat of paint they might never see till all the wood turned silver, and the house was almost indistinguishable from the trees and fields.

As he bends beneath the cellar rafters, spider webs tighten across his outstretched hands. He reaches for the small lightbulb overhead, threading it in tight with his fingertips till he crouches in his own

DWELLING

shadow. Rusted garden tools, burlap sacks chewed apart by mice, cloudy blue Mason jars with corroded caps, broken clay flower pots, strands of wire, old animal traps, part of a deer hide, and a pile of antlers locked like a puzzle lay scattered about the cellar, remnants of a dark past Jack never found the will to abandon at the local dump.

Hope disliked the cellar, its dampness, the noises, the creatures that crawled around in the dark—mice, silverfish, spiders, the snakes lying on the bottom steps in summer, the porcupine that got in last fall and chewed the centerpost. Jack never remembering to hook the cellar door shut. Much of her anxieties over the house she attributed to something down there. That's where the mice came in, the ants, the spiders, the cold air. That time Jack was gone and she had to go down to the cellar alone one night to change a fuse, and a bird or a bat or something came flying overhead, trapped in the dark. How she screamed.

Now with the new furnace, the rewiring for the thermostat, the fusebox moved to the back porch, the cellar seldom concerned her. That the temperature down there no longer perserved her garden produce seemed yet another abnormality of the place. She rid her mind of the cellar almost entirely.

Hope stands on the walk with a basket of freshly picked green beans in each hand and notices the cellar door open, hears him making noises down there.

Jack? Did you fix it? It's getting colder. I need my heavier jacket. Come up when you're through and take your pills. I'll leave them on the table.

If you asked her, she would say Jack is in retreat.

THE GHOST OF SANDBURG'S PHIZZOG

Her husband is not himself and hasn't been for some time. He was an ambitious advertising man in their early years of marriage, self-sufficient, given to long working hours, solitary drinking and occasional affairs. He was once that. He was a man who expressed his feelings awkwardly and rarely divulged anything that absorbed his attention. Not to me, anyway, thought Hope. Maybe to others. If she was jealous of anything, it was the extent and depth to which Jack may have shared his heart with other lovers but never revealed it to her. She found it difficult to even imagine him that way. What did he do? What did he say? She knew him as a good provider. Dutiful. A caring father. It was simply enough when he came to her those nights in silence, his body expressing some dense need. A need, to her, that became even greater in time as he began to fade before a realness of daily life he could no longer bear.

There was just too much out there that could neither be explained or understood, he confessed to her once during a siege of disorientation. While she had made the adjustment to the country for his well-being, it did not seem an equitable trade-off. Jack had lost ground, never regained his old self. She could no longer distinguish between silence or depression in him. Her responsibility now shifted to sickness and health: to refill the doctor's prescriptions and keep him busy for his own good.

I'm going back to the garden, Jack, she says. I've put the thermostat down where it was and turned the oven off. Maybe you should call the heating man. Don't forget your pills. Make a sandwich for yourself for lunch. I'm going to pick as much as I can. There's going to be a hard frost tonight. Give

DWELLING

me a hand when you're through down there.

He checks the connection box and fuel line, the damper on the pipe leading to the chimney. His hands are covered with soot. He pushes the red re-set button on the furnace motor, vaguely expecting some kind of explosion, and when nothing happens, unscrews the burning lightbulb and crouches toward the cellar wall, leaning against it to relieve his cramped body, gradually slumping till he rests upon the bedrock floor, stretching his legs in front of him. Closing his eyes, huddled within his jacket, he perceives the problem to be one of temperature. Inside and out. Uneven. The thermostat upstairs which Hope always begins fooling with in early fall when the house must make a seasonal adjustment. As the day starts to wane, the air outside turns colder, the furnace should kick in. He curls his hands around the traps in the pockets of his jacket, and slowly begins playing them in unison with the tips of his fingers, discovering a rhythm, maintaining it. He picks up his own heart beat.

Later when Hope returns, he is still in the cellar. His legs folded beneath him, his back straight, free of the wall. Through the opening of the cellar door, the light is deeper gray, the color of the mole.

Jack, are you still down there? What's the matter? Jack?

She is tempted to open the door with her foot, tentatively, the way one might turn over a dead bird with the toe of his shoe, but no, she will not go down there. She will not go down there and find him dead, find him overdosed, or hung, or electrocuted by the furnace. He is in the house. Sleeping in his chair.

Jack? she calls into the dark kitchen. Jack? He is

THE GHOST OF SANDBURG'S PHIZZOG

not in the living room. The house is cold, but not as cold as it is turning outside. The pills are still on the table. She sits there at the window and watches the trees, the garden, the field, the road, gradually lose shape as the glass begins to fog from her breath, and the day darken. She hears the late calls of birds. But nothing from down there.

She should call for help, the sheriff, the doctor, someone, but she does not want to make a scene. Especially over nothing. If he is out on one of his long walks. And he should come walking through the door. At the same time he is dead. And she is relieved, and finds that unexplainable. He is her husband. Someone she loved. She is empty and still for a long while.

And then a noise from the cellar. A humming.

Jack? she mouths his name. Oh Jack, she whispers.

In his lap he worries each point of a tangle of antlers till his fingertips are numb. When the sound of a cry drifts down from above, he extends a hand toward the furnace, feeling for the motor's shape, finding and pressing the button, re-set. The furnace fires.

Closing his eyes, his body resonates in a moaning deep and familiar, indistinguishable from pain or craving, desiring a simplest response: the sound returned, the forms consumed, the tears touched.

On the kitchen window wet with steam, Hope has drawn a childish heart in Jack's name, with an arrow only halfway through before it all begins to run in one clear stream down the sill.

She places the tip of her wet finger first to her eyes, then to his lips.

The Chair Trick

The thick pile of the funeral-parlor rug brushes my face. I hear Punchocar's voice, see his gray gabardine coat. There is a broken button like a half-moon on the sleeve. Thumbs pressed into my shoulders, he stuffs me into a metal folding chair in the middle row—between him and Sylvia Kanvalinka. Their shoulders support me.

"Take it easy," whispers my father from across the aisle. "Be still."

Gertie is sobbing. Horak, the funeral director, is upset. Folding chairs are strewn all around the casket. The wrong chairs. You need straight-back wooden ones; you can't work with these damn things.

"Oh, Gertie, for Christ's sake, shut up!" I shout.

Punchocar puts his arm around me, and Sylvia places my hand on her perfectly round, nyloned knee. Her hand pats mine.

"Murph's down," I whisper. He is flat on his back in the casket—the first time I have ever seen him down.

"Somebody should say something about Murph and the chairs," I say. "Huh, Punchocar?"

"Sh-h-h," says Ma, turning around in the front row. "You're making a fool of yourself.

Murph was married to Gertie, Ma's sister, which made him a distant relation at best. He was a constant guest but never a true member of our tribe. Not a Slav, only an Irishman—a lazy Irishman, as Ma would say. He did not speak our language, eat our food, dance our dances. He smoked Lucky Strikes. He drank only Schlitz and Jim Beam—to excess. He made everyone but Gertie feel good.

He was tall and lean, and as self-composed as a mannequin in a department-store window. There was a matter-of-factness about his presence. He worked in the office of the Hector Gasket Company, where he was in charge of accounts, and when I was a child he saved empty wooden spools from his adding machine for me. Once, he built a tower of them higher than I could reach. It fell when Ma brushed against it accidentally, though she had warned us that it was too high and that it would inevitably fall by itself.

He was a gambler, and once dealt for Capone's brother at the old 4811 Club in Cicero. My father said he could have been a C.P.A. if only he had had the ambition. Numbers did not lie—Murph knew that, but he preferred luck.

"What do you have there, Murph?" I remember him showing my father a piece of paper like onionskin with three horses printed on it, each with a dark line leading to the word "Finish." Behind the horses was a black star.

"Which one do you want?" asked Murph.

We each picked a horse. Murph put the hot tip of his Lucky Strike to the star, setting off the horses in a slow but burning streak to the finish line. The remainder of the paper never caught fire—only the star, the horses, and their path to the end.

Murph won, laughing, and crumbled the paper in an ashtray like a dry leaf. He brushed his hands, wiped them on a folded white handkerchief, then reached inside his breast pocket for a fresh stack of horse races.

"I've got a quarter riding on No. 3 this time," he said.

THE CHAIR TRICK

Then Murph and Ma. Murph telling a Bob Hope joke to her alone in the kitchen, leaning against the sink. "Lu," he says, tugging his nose, pulling his chin, hiking up his pants. "You should have heard Hope on the radio the time he told about the woman and her hands—"

"Go on. I've heard that. Get away from me," Ma says, laughing as Murph moves closer. "Gertie! Watch this old man of yours," she hollers toward the parlor. "Be careful or I'll drop this platter."

"He makes such a fool out of me," Gertie whimpers later to Ma in the pantry. "Little pitchers have big ears," she adds, waving a finger at me.

Settled on each end of the sofa, Murph and Father are drinking beer in the parlor, brown bottles of Schlitz between their legs. I have carried nine empty bottles back to the kitchen for Murph, two for my father. Half a bottle of Jim Beam and a shot glass rest on the end table alongside Murph. Sunday afternoon. The world on an even keel. Murph stands to light a Lucky. He is not comfortable sitting down.

"I'm going to leave him," Gertie says.

"Why don't you?" says Ma.

"And then what? Then what?"

"The doctor comes in the room with this beautiful nurse to check on a patient who's supposed to be dying," Murph tells my father. " 'Hell, there's life in him yet,' says the doc. 'How can you ...' "

"He doesn't sleep," says Gertie. "He hates to sleep. He's at the tavern every night. His supper gets cold. I don't know what to do."

"I'd give him his supper," says Ma. "Right over his head."

Gertie was someone to feel sorry for. Though we

might have entertained the thought of her finally leaving Murph, we knew it was all talk. Husbands and wives just lived together forever. And when Murph finally died, from a bad liver, Gertie began crying how she missed him, how good he was. She rode the city buses day and night, getting lost in subways and odd neighborhoods, afraid to go home to her empty flat. She swore that the ghost of Murph visited her standing on its head upon a kitchen chair. That must have been on her mind more and more after he was gone.

At World Series time, in October, I would come home from school and Murph would usually be there visiting, watching the game on TV. He always took his vacation at that time, because he knew the New York Yankees would be playing. Though he came from the Irish South Side, a stronghold of White Sox fans, Murph loved the Yankees and old Casey Stengel. Once, though, when school let out at noon, and I came home earlier than usual, Ma made me hide in the pantry with her, pretending not to be home, while Murph stood out on the back porch pressing the doorbell, hollering, "Lu! Hey, Lu! It's me. Open up."

That was when Ma told me that white lies were all right. My father didn't believe in any lies at all. And he would never say anything like what Ma said to Gertie at Punchocar's twenty-fifth wedding anniversary: "If you can't trust him, Gertie, get rid of him." People just never upset him that way. Everything would get better with time. Forgiveness and forgetfullness were the same.

Ma could say whatever she wanted about Gertie's

THE CHAIR TRICK

marriage to Murph, about how inconsiderate Murph was, and my father would be quick to remind her how Murph always helped at church carnivals and bingo games, how he took time off before Christmas to work on the truck that made the neighborhood rounds collecting old toys for children in the orphanages. "Yes, and drunk all the while," said Ma.

Drunkenness was no doubt his cross, though he carried it well inside of himself. There was never a hesitancy to his steps. There was a neatness and sureness to him, and then a silence unending. I never saw him fall of his own accord. He was not a crawler, or even a man who sought the stability of his knees in prayer. He stood through each Mass at the back of the church.

Families and lovers have histories all their own, but distant relations forever remain intrusions. I can no more imagine Murph romancing Gertie than I can picture a stranger coming into the kitchen and making love to Ma every afternoon, once a year, when the Yankees played in the World Series.

As I grew older, I left the neighborhood, went away to college, married, divorced. I would find my way home occasionally for the comfort of finding everything else in place. My father was still passive, kind, accepting. Ma as outspoken as ever, still implying that Murph's antics were intolerable, though I had known, since that time I came home early, that they were lovers. As a child, I honored the secret, fearing that its divulgence might result in the loss of all: Father, Ma, and Murph. As a grown man, discovering my weaknesses, I honored whatever

THE GHOST OF SANDBURG'S PHIZZOG

manner of marriage my parents had made for themselves, and I feared the loss of Murph, which I still cannot explain, and the loss of myself. I knew only that I still had all three of them, and I wanted to hear more of Ma's tales about Murph.

"He doesn't want to listen to that," my father would say. But Ma could never leave any story untold. Stories began and ended within my father. Ma had to let go of the words. She was the embroiderer, the puller of stitches, the unknotter of thread. Every year brought a falling-out with one relation or another. People in her hands met a steady unravelling. First, she would go for the laugh. Then, if she was jealous, she would go for the hurt.

"Now, you don't know that for sure." My father would try to reason with her.

"Well, it's true!" Ma would laugh, anxious to go on with it. "Murph was so drunk last week that he left the tavern around midnight with his two buddies, Eddie Holub and that other drunk, Punchocar, and they picked up Sylvia Kanvalinka, that divorced one who sleeps with anybody, and they all went to the airport in a cab and flew to Las Vegas! Poor Gertie couldn't understand what happened to him. She had the police out and everything..." Ma broke into laughter again. Father tried not to smile, then joined in the laughter because it was so hearty, so infectious. "So he finally calls Gertie the next morning. 'Mommy,' he says, 'what's for supper? I'm in Las Vegas. I'll be back tonight.' Oh, I'd give him Las Vegas," said Ma, gesturing with her hand. "I'd kill the son of a bitch!"

"He probably wasn't even there," said my father, who would never ask Murph about it. "He probably stayed over at Punchocar's."

THE CHAIR TRICK

"What do you mean he wasn't there? Of course he was there. Are you calling me a liar? Gertie will show you the damn ticket." She turned to me. "You know your father. He doesn't believe anything I tell him."

The day of Murph's funeral, I found a chair in the back row of Horak's Funeral Parlor, fell into it, and waited for everyone to arrive. When Punchocar showed up, I went next door and had a few drinks with him. Returning to the parlor, I met Sylvia going in and talked her into going next door for a drink.

"This is the way Murph would have liked it," she said. She was old stuff but always new. Either her hair was done up differently or she was dressed in a way no one had ever seen before. She told me that the trip to Las Vegas with Murph was one of the few good memories in her life. "Our feet never touched the ground," she said.

When we returned to the funeral parlor, my folks were there. Father motioned to me, and I joined him near the back of the room. Ma was up front comforting Gertie.

"I can't imagine Murph flat on his back like that," I told him.

"Yes, well..."

I milled among the friends and relatives who began to fill the place with their talk and laughter. I went next door for a few beers with Father, and then again, a little later, with Punchocar. There was a steady coming and going of the men.

Gertie sat in place, sobbing, receiving much sympathy from the women. The men did not know what to say, so shook her hand instead. No one paid

much attention to me as I began pulling a few chairs behind me, assembling them in front of the casket.

I got only as far as the second tier when my foot got caught in the folding seat and the whole thing came down. Horak collared me, dumping me into the hands of Punchocar, who had seen the chair trick done right many times before.

It was at Punchocar's twenty-fifth wedding anniversary that Murph had perfected the trick. Over a hundred people—family and friends, plus a few dozen kids—packed Pilsen Hall, where all our celebrations were held. There was a five-piece polka band: two button-box concertinas, a clarinet, a tamburitza, and a drum. Punchocar, with a bald head and red butcher's hands, danced his big wife, Mileko, under the silver paper bell that hung above the dance floor. Streamers of paper dollars rained down. Punchocar, a circle dancer of great skill, guided Mileko through the steps so smoothly there was rhythm enough in his hands to gently pat the bottom of every other woman who came near.

Even Murph was dancing.

"Just look at him," Gertie said as he returned from the dance floor with Ma. Ma was laughing so hard she kept falling into him.

"Murph," Father said, and he motioned with his head. "Sylvia over there wants to dance." It was one of my father's habits at such celebrations to see that everyone was enjoying himself—especially Murph.

"Sit down already," said Gertie as Murph pushed away from the table and headed for Sylvia.

Sylvia Kanvalinka was twice divorced, a distant relation come back to the neighborhood to begin life anew. She had dark skin, dark eyes, blond hair, high

THE CHAIR TRICK

cheekbones. Her grandfather was pure Hungarian, they said, and gypsy, rumor had it. Though she was spreading softly with middle age, Sylvia retained a hard beauty. A little heavy in the thighs, but bosomy enough for the men of the tribe. She had everyone's attention on this occasion, and was danced and romanced to death by all the old Serbs and Croatians. Punchocar himself led the pack until Murph stepped onto the dance floor—the Irish jig in his legs, and his head held straight and high—and lifted Sylvia into shouting leaps of polka.

"I never knew he could dance like that," said Father.

"She's just a whore," said Ma.

"There he goes, making a damn fool of me again," said Gertie.

Murph danced most of the night with Sylvia. Later, when some of the people were beginning to leave, and when the bar was no longer busy, my father smiled and nudged Ma. "Look, there goes Murph with the chairs." It was almost time for the band to begin playing "Good Night, Ladies."

"I'm going," said Gertie, heading toward the cloakroom to get her things.

I saw myself on the threshold of young manhood that night. Leaving the others at the table, I began gathering the chairs for Murph.

"I'll get the band for you," I told him. And he nodded. "Let's have your coat," I said.

He rolled up his sleeves, moved the arrow clasp to the bottom of his tie and rubbed his chin. "Wait," he said. "I think I'll try a table this time." Together we moved an empty banquet table to the dance floor.

"When we get all the chairs together," I in-

111

structed the band, "I'll give you the signal. He needs a drumroll. Keep an eye on him. When he's finished, then you can go into your 'Good Night, Ladies.'"

Usually he did it with a pyramid of six chairs. But he took ten chairs this time, which meant he had to stack them four tiers high upon a table. He easily lined the first four chairs straight across and secured three chairs on top of them. The next two took some reaching and climbing.

There was no helping Murph from this point on. Those who tried were politely told to get out of his way, and if they didn't they faced the prospect of Murph standing dead still in the space he had cleared for himself until the privacy of his act was acknowledged.

The final chair, the very point of the pyramid, took the most time for him to set up. He carefully climbed up on the second tier, testing it, then the third, grasping the chair seats in both hands, testing again the solidness of the footing. Then he moved down backward, grabbed the last chair in one hand, and extended it away from him till he had climbed high enough to put it in place at the top. He would never know how firm the final chair was until he committed himself to it.

I signaled for the drumroll.

Gertie, in coat and hat, waited in a far corner of the hall. Murphy took the white handkerchief from his back pocket, wiped his forehead, then suddenly broke his concentration when he saw her wave. He emptied his pockets into Sylvia's hands.

Another drumroll. I returned to our table to watch.

Murph began in the middle of the first row, one

THE CHAIR TRICK

foot on each of the two center chairs. He paused dramatically and snapped his fingers for another drumroll. A few people began to clap.

He started with his left foot toward the second tier, then firmly planted his other foot in place to an accompaniment of *ta-dah!* from the band, a few whistles, and some applause.

The third tier, of two chairs, took greater concentration. He removed his shoes, letting them drop with little regard. He proceeded cautiously in his black-stockinged feet, right foot first, then the left. More applause. People were gathering beneath him now.

His act was usually complete at this level. He would stand still, raise both arms over his head, then bring them down slowly till they extended at his sides as if he were encompassing everything in space, while the people below whistled, clapped, shouted, and the band went into "Good Night, Ladies."

This time, with the additional chairs, it was obvious that he would attempt something more. Women began covering their eyes, peeking between their fingers. The men in the bar assembled into a group by the doorway. As Murph leaned into the top chair for steadiness, Gertie bid him goodbye. "You're a damn fool! I've been crazy to put up with you all these years!"

People laughed and told her to be still.

"You don't have to live with this," she told them. "You don't know what it means to be married to such a fool. What it does to you." And then she was gone.

In the silence of his approach to the last chair, it became evident, even from where I stood, that

Murph was in new territory. His arms and legs seemed to tremble.

He gripped the top chair tightly in both hands and proceeded, little by little, to lift his body till he stood on his head and seemingly disappeared in the darkness beyond the light.

He was awarded loud applause and shrill whistles while the band moved unexpectedly from a final drumroll to a rousing "For He's a Jolly Good Fellow." Murph remained in place through it all, until the band slid softly into "Good Night, Ladies" and the dancers and well-wishers moved closer to welcome his descent.

"What the hell does he think he's trying to do?" said Ma. We moved from our table to the dance floor. My father squeezed his way up front and stood next to Sylvia. Then Ma and I shoved our way through till we stood directly in line with the chairs, pressing our shoulders back to keep others from pushing us into the table.

Everyone looked upward, straining, feeling dizzy, trying to catch Murph.

"You'll break your neck, and then what?" yelled Ma.

People began to turn away from him, making excuses to go home, freeing themselves of responsibility.

"Be careful!" shouted my father to one man stumbling near the chairs. "You want to get somebody killed?" He grabbed him by the neck and hurled him back into the crowd.

Sylvia emerged, stood smiling up at Murph's antics, shielding her eyes from the light. My father gently guided the small of her back. "Can you see

THE CHAIR TRICK

me, Murph?" she said, reaching with both hands, quietly pressing her fingertips toward him.

It was a small movement at first. It began in his shoulders. Just one twitch. Followed by another, which tore along his side to his knees. Murph brought his ankles closer together and stretched his toes toward the pressed-tin ceiling and the round, milk-white chandeliers that seemed to swing from the heavens like moons on indiscernible chains. He was never coming down.

Ma turned back abruptly and gave way, fully certain of Murph's inevitable return to earth and of the unsteadiness of all men, even her own flesh and blood.

This Horse of a Body of Mine

Mother is dying of cancer the doctors say, and I am in a state of remission. I am driving her home from my place in Wisconsin in my father's 1965 Oldsmobile four-door sedan with 35,000 miles on it, original tires, spotless interior, and two coats of Simonize he hand-rubbed the day before we left. The chrome bumpers glisten. The engine, valve covers, and air cleaner shine. The spare tire, wrapped in plastic, has never touched the ground. My father believes if you take good care of things they will last the rest of your life.

Once a year, when I pick mother up for a brief vacation with us, I leave my car in the garage and drive the Oldsmobile up north to burn the carbon out. "Look at all that rust on the body," he says. "You don't take care of things." Once a year I always ask him to join mother and me to visit my wife and kids in Wisconsin, but he has no desire to go anywhere. "It's too far. There's nothing to do. I've got plenty to keep me busy around here," he says.

"How's the car running?" I ask.

"Pretty good. It keeps stopping in wet weather, so I had the guy down the alley tune it up for me."

"That's because you don't use it. It's full of carbon again."

"Once it's warmed up, it's fine. The fellow at the gas station wants to give me five hundred for it. Are you kidding? I said. It's like new. There's nothing like a good heavy car under you in an accident. You don't have a chance in that car of yours."

"You should take yours on the highway once a month. All you do is drive it to the store and church and back."

"And drive your mother shopping. If it wasn't for

her, I wouldn't even have a car. I can walk wherever I go. She can't even walk to the corner."

The Olds is filled with the scent of Estée Lauder, her favorite perfume. "Such an old fashioned car," she says, sitting beside me on the wide front seat, fumbling with the radio and cigarette lighter. "Look at this ashtray. Did you ever see an ashtry like this? Brand new. He has a fit if I dirty it. I have to carry my own ashtry in my purse when he drives. Did you ever hear of such a thing? He keeps pennies in there for parking meters. What the hell are you saving it for? I tell him. I tell you, that father of yours."

She is eating from a bag of Jonathan apples we just purchased at a roadside market. Fresh fruit is good for her, my wife says. Fresh fruit, no white flour, no sugar or salt. Natural vitamins and exercise. She's too fat. You have to talk to her doctor about mega-vitamins whether he listens to you or not. Look what they've done for you. Doctors don't know anything about nutrition.

I don't know for sure that vitamins and natural foods did anything for me. I know I took months of radiation treatment for my kind of cancer, and then Doctor Sedlack, the family doctor, said it looks good, and I have been living in a state of remission for over five years now, which Sedlack says is another good sign. Sheryl believes the side effects of radiation are dangerous, that I've been burned, and that I should never let them do that to me, especially since Sedlack is nothing but a general practitioner.

"Sedlack has been our doctor for as long as I can remember," I tell her. "He speaks my mother's native tongue. She calls him all hours of the day and

night. He even comes to the house. She jokes with him. She gives him something to eat. She loves Doctor Sedlack."

"I don't care," says my wife. "If you want her to die, let her keep listening to those people with their radiation and their chemotherapy. They're going to kill her."

"She won't listen to me," I tell her.

"Well, she's your mother," she replies.

"He never plays the radio when he drives," my mother says, biting into another apple, humming with the music.

"You should eat more fruit like that," I tell her. "Lay off all the sweets."

"Everything bothers him. Who wants to listen to all that noise? he moans. What a treat to be able to sit back, light a cigarette, listen to the radio, and watch all these beautiful farms go by. He never wants to go anywhere. If it wasn't for me, he'd die in that house. Look at all these small cars on the highway. When I get back I'm going to tell him to buy a new car. What's the name of that small one there? Something like that. Something like yours. Who the hell wants these big monsters anymore?"

"I could never get your father to do anything," she says, kicking off her white shoes. "Oh these damn feet keep swelling up. Sedlack says it's all water, it's nothing to worry about. He gave me some pills. I've got more damn pills. Who the hell knows?" She's rummaging through her straw purse for some hard candy and a tube of lipstick. "Your father's always been a stick-in-the-mud. Don't forget I want to stop for some smoked fish and some cheese. You want some candy? They're good. They're hot. Let's stop

in one of these small towns for breakfast. I always took my vacations alone. You're better off."

She pulls the sun visor down to arrange her platinum blonde wig in the mirror and put on fresh lipstick. She retains an attractiveness that has demanded attention all her life. Beneath the layers of makeup is an old peasant face, my grandmother's, that I have rarely glimpsed and only noticed emerge for the first time in the hospital the past year. She is wearing a bright floral dress, pink, white, violet and blue. Her wrinkled fingers are thick with costume jewelry. She is wearing an extravagant gold looking necklace and bracelet I gave her after her recent operation, fixing it around her neck and upon her wrist while she was dressed in a hospital gown and being fed intravenously. "I hope he remembers to take the pork loin out of the freezer for supper," she says.

She should not be eating pork, according to Sheryl. "All her life she's eaten poisons. Nothing but nitrates. All that homemade sausage from the butcher, tripe soup, lamb, chicken paprika," she says "Bakery, booze, and cigarettes. Then she wonders why she's got cancer. She thinks it's going to go away just like that. Your father doesn't even mention the word in front of her. She doesn't have to eat for two months, with all that fat on her. Tell your father not to buy that stuff. She should be eating more raw vegetables."

"She gets through with supper," says my father, "and after coffee, bakery, and cigarettes, she makes herself an ice cream sundae. She doesn't want people to think she looks sick. What am I going to do with her? Starve her? She won't listen to me. The doctors say all that vitamin business is the bunk. What am I

supposed to tell Sedlack? They want to try radiation, so they try it. Then they cut her open again and say they can't do anymore surgery, and now chemotherapy is what she should have. The odds are one in five. I don't even tell your mother this. They must know what they're doing. They're doctors. If they cut it all out, why isn't it gone?"

To listen to my wife, I should take my mother to some place out east where they cleanse the body of toxins and prescribe a diet of wheat grass. The body's metabolism must be turned around to cure its own disease. Or I should get her off chemotherapy immediately and fly her to Mexico for laetrile treatment in some clinic on the Pacific.

"Get out of here," says my mother. "Me on a plane? I'd sooner crawl. So what's supposed to happen to me anyway? Will you tell me? My fingernails are supposed to fall off, my hair's supposed to fall out. Will you please tell me what this stuff is doing to me every week? I've gained fifteen pounds since the last operation. So what am I supposed to turn green or something? Nothing phases me. Not this horse of a body of mine."

On Water Street in the town of Kewa Bay we park beside a small corner restaurant. Mother pulls out a pair of pink felt house slippers from her shopping bag and shoves her swollen feet into them. "What the hell do these farmers know?" she says. They are the same style of house slipper my grandmother wore all her life. She pushes the car door open with her knee and bangs it into a parking meter. "Can't they put those damn things somewhere else out of the way?" Standing in the bright sun, she puts on a pair of dark sun glasses and places a white straw picture

hat on the back of her head, fixing it with a pearl hatpin.

"This place is too crowded," she says at the door of the restaurant. The tables and counter are filled with fishermen from all over Wisconsin and Illinois who have come to catch some coho salmon in fall. The bay is smooth and silver in the distance, studded with fishing boats drifting in the early morning mist and sun. "There's a bakery over there," she says. "I'll get some sweetrolls and bread and coffeecake to take home for supper."

I watch the bulk of her shift from side to side in small steps toward the bakery, stopping to peer into a clothing store window along the way. She is the brightest thing on the street this morning.

Dressed in a blue and white running suit and gray running shoes, I fix a red bandanna on my head and call out to her that I will jog along the lakeshore while she shops. "Don't get all tired out," she says.

Though I married outside of the church, much of my adult life echoes a Catholic upbringing. I am more aware now of abstinence, penance, suffering. When my wife suggested fasting once a week for reasons of health, she could barely comprehend my familiarity with abstinence long ago — fish on Friday, Lenten fasts, never eating on Sundays before taking the sacrament of Holy Communion. Running, in my mind, is penance, suffering, and prayer. I fast for her now for reasons of good health. I have lost my priests. The nuns have become indistinguishable from other women.

"Once a week," says my wife, "the body needs a rest. Once a week we will eat nothing." Today is my fast day.

THIS HORSE OF A BODY OF MINE

Driving toward Milwaukee, the monotony of the interstate taking hold, I feel my body relaxing, my mind slipping into sleep. "You look tired," she says. "Don't fall asleep now." She turns the radio up louder and offers me a piece of bakery again.

"No thanks," I say. "I'm not eating today. You should try that. Just not eat anything one day a week. You'll feel better."

"Here, try one of these almond crescents. I'll split it with you."

"No. You eat it."

"I don't need it. You look all drawn out. Your face is too thin."

"I feel fine."

"You can't live on nothing. You hardly eat anything in that house of yours."

She takes one bite of the almond crescent and throws the rest back into the bag. "They sure as hell don't know what good bakery is around here."

"Why don't you take a nap, mother? We still have a few more hours to drive."

"I've got all night to sleep."

"You want to look through some magazines? There are some on the back seat."

"Just drive. Don't worry about me."

"Try the radio near the end of the dial. Sometimes you can find polka music."

She turns her shoulder to me slightly, lights another cigarette, and looks out the window, retreating to a stubborn silence I remember as a child.

"Do you still want to stop for some smoked fish? It's up ahead a few miles."

"No, just get me home already. Christ, this is a long ride."

THE GHOST OF SANDBURG'S PHIZZOG

She begins digging into her purse for her rosary and prayer book stuffed with holy cards, all wrapped with one of the wide rubberbands my father saves on the kitchen doorknobs. She turns to the page of indulgenced ejaculations, moving her lips in the words of the last indulgence: *Mother of love, of sorrow, and of mercy, pray for us.* For each utterance, a remission of 300 days of temporal punishment is granted by the church.

I smile in her persistence of such old beliefs, in my own childhood attempts to pile up indulgences at odd moments to lessen my soul's stay in purgatory. She wraps the beads around her hand like old bakery string to be saved and tied and put in the kitchen drawer. It is the same rosary I bought her in Rome, supposedly blessed by her beloved Pope John. She makes the sign of the cross, then works her fingers and lips from the crucifix to the Our Father, the Hail Mary, and the First Joyful Mystery, the Annunciation. She brushes some flakes of frosting from her lap, and beneath the necklace on her bosom, retrieves a large crumb which she places in her mouth.

"Your family still believes that eating cures everything," say my wife. "Your aunts are killing their husbands, loading their plates every meal, stuffing them with rye bread and butter, filling their glasses with beer. Then bakery on top of all that. No wonder the whole family suffers from diabetes and heart trouble, and now cancer. Your grandmother could hardly move, she was so huge. Your mother's getting just like her. How can you educate those people? Your mother still believes fat babies are healthy. My children were always too skinny for her."

THIS HORSE OF A BODY OF MINE

Our children, slim and supple as young branches, are runners, ten-speed bikers, cross-country skiers, hikers with aluminum-framed backpacks, down vests, jackets, and sleeping bags. They dress in bright colored warm-up gear and survive on small portions of nutritious meals, home-baked wheat bread, fresh juice, raw vegetables, brown rice, vitamins, exercise, and sneak occasional junk food in the company of their friends. They can't wait till they are of age to leave home for the summer, camp in wilderness areas alone, climb mountains, and go whitewater rafting in the West. They have little to say about their grandmother, who embarrasses them with the smelly food she cooks, the perfume she exudes, the queer clothes she wears, the lipstick smeared kisses she tries to plant on their cheeks. They think she comes from another world.

"All she does is try to stuff them with candy and bakery and salty food," says my wife, "then gives them money to buy anything they want. That's not love. Like married to your father over 40 years and always arguing. You call that a marriage?"

At Hanson's Fish and Cheese Shop I leave mother in the car saying her rosary and buy five pounds of smoked chubs, and a pound each of Baby Swiss, munster, and brick. While the woman is wrapping the fish in newspaper, mother walks in and begins tasting the tiny chunks of cheese set on a tray for customers to sample.

"What is this?" she asks.

"A cheese curd," says the woman.

"That's good. Give us a pound of curds. And a slice of this aged cheddar too. Oh, about that much, a couple of inches. Father likes caraway. You better

THE GHOST OF SANDBURG'S PHIZZOG

give us a pound of cheddar with caraway also."

While the woman is weighing and wrapping the cheese, mother adds a box of crackers, some diet cola, and a handful of hard salami sticks wrapped in plastic.

Back on the highway, she is nibbling on cheese curds with crackers and drinking from a can of diet cola. "I've got crumbs all over. This car's a mess. Your father's going to kill us. The next time you come in, bring a couple cartons of these curds. They're delicious. Your Aunt Milada would like them. Wait till father sees this smoked fish. Remember how we used to eat smoked fish every Friday?"

A few miles before the expressway through Milwaukee she asks me to stop somewhere so she can use the restroom. There are no rest areas along the interstate or expressway, I tell her. I will have to get off and take the old highway that parallels the new interstate. I remember a small wayside along that stretch.

The old highway is empty and in need of repair. We bump along the tar cracks in the concrete, mother periodically exclaiming, "Jesus, what kind of a road is this?" Yet the road brings us in closer to the farms, closer to the animals and fields and trees.

"All these beautiful farms with red barns," she says. "Look at those cows, and those baby pigs. Aren't they cute! Remember Grandma's farm in Three Oaks? How she killed the chickens for supper? And the butter she used to make? God, how she worked herself to death on that farm."

We are the only car in the parking lot of the wayside. While mother trudges toward the restroom, I push the front seat back, stretch, and close my eyes.

"Just rest," she says when she returns. "I'm going

THIS HORSE OF A BODY OF MINE

to get rid of some of this garbage and pump some cold well water over there."

It is early afternoon. I can feel the burning sun on my eyelids. The country smells of drying grasses, cedar, the end of summer. I hear the quick then slow squeaks of the pump handle, then the sudden rush of water. From the corner of my eye I catch a blurry glimpse of her sitting at a green picnic table, her face turned up into the sun, her skirt hiked above her knees, tanning her heavy legs.

I awake to hunger pains, growling sounds. Opening my eyes I discover my head resting against her thigh, while her head hangs above me in a snoring sleep. The blonde wig has fallen to the floor. Gray hair is matted against her forehead and lies bunched above her ears. Her face is as ancient as Grandma's. Rumblings inside her body echo mine, though hers emanate from the pelvic region, where her hands lay clasped, where her cancer lies.

Grasping the steering wheel, I pull myself up slowly.

"What's wrong?" her eyes flash open.

"Nothing. I want to splash some cold water on my face, then we better get going."

"Here, put some water in this empty soda can for me. I like that iron taste of well water. It reminds me of Grandma's farm and the picnics we used to go on a long time ago in the forest preserves."

I return to find her staring at her face in the mirror behind the visor, her hands vaguely stirring inside her purse. "I look like hell," she says. "Just look at me." She opens a tube of lipstick, then a compact of facial coloring which she rubs deep into her skin. "Hand me that damn wig," she says. She brushes it

with her hand, fluffing the piles of blonde curls with her fingers. "There. That's good enough." I hand her the can of cold well water. "Oh, that tastes good," she says. "We should fill up a gallon jug to take home."

All the way back through Milwaukee and over the Illinois state line she talks about her childhood, the picnics they used to go to in the forest preserves. "Grandpa belonged to this club, Ilova, named after some place in Yugoslavia, and they would hold these picnics every year. A truck would come for us early in the morning, and we would all pile on, the kids, the old people, everyone. The trucks were open in the back with those wooden sides, and we would sit there on top of one another and drive all the way to the picnic grounds outside the city.

"Sometimes we would carry blocks of ice with us too in burlap sacks. Grandpa and some of the men would leave even earlier to begin building the fires so they could start roasting lambs and pigs on the spit. They would rub the lambs and pigs both inside and out with handfuls of salt. Sometimes they would stuff the cavities with sausage, and sometimes they would slit the outside skin of the lamb and stick cloves of garlic inside. Grandma would be with the women making coffee, cutting bread, setting out the bakery. Grandpa would later end up with his friends drinking beer and playing cards. The kids would take turns turning the lambs and the pigs on the spit by hand. Then the band would begin playing in the afternoon, and everyone would sing and dance till night. Most of the men would be drunk by then, and the women would be battling with them. Then they would all pile on the trucks and go home, their bellies full.

"You never tasted lamb like that. So juicy. They'd cut and saw and chop it apart. They were no butchers, believe me. You didn't bother with forks. You ate with your hands like a bunch of savages. The skin of the pig was so nice and brown and crispy you could just crack it between your teeth or chew on it all day if you wanted to."

"I ate roast lamb like that in Greece," I tell her. "They still make it that way outside on the spit during Greek Easter."

"Well, they don't have picnics like that anymore," she says. "I don't know what happened to Ilova. They must be all dead."

"Doesn't anyone in the neighborhood roast lambs like that? The Greeks? The Serbs? There must be some Croatian picnics still."

"The young people don't go for that. There's this new Yugoslav butcher, Luka, where I sometimes get my meat. He's supposed to sell lamb and suckling pig he roasts in the back every week. But I don't know if it's against the law nowadays or not."

"Well, ask him when you buy your meat."

"What time is it? Go down Cermak when we get to the neighborhood. I'll just run in and see if he's got anything."

As we approach the outskirts of Chicago, I hear her rummaging through her purse again, her hands tearing the cellophane wrapper off the salami snack. She finishes one. Opens another. Takes a bite out of it and passes it to me. "Here, take a bite. It's good."

I pretend to taste it and pass it back.

"You didn't even try it," she says, crumbling the cellophane into the ashtray.

"Father's probably wondering where we're at," I say to her.

"Let him wonder. All he's going to do is tell me how hard he worked while I was on vacation. How he washed the windows, scrubbed the floor, painted the storm windows. Get the fiddle. Same old stuff. Or he's in the alley. Garbage picking. Bringing home more junk, fixing it, then trying to get rid of it. He can hardly get the car in the garage, he's got so much junk in there. Now he found a guy down the alley throwing out good shoes. He worked for some shoe company or something. Seconds. Shoes people sent back. So your father, you know how he loves to polish shoes and visit the shoemaker. The garage is filled with shoes. He gave five pair to Uncle John last week and one pair to some other guy down the alley. He wants me to ask Sedlack what size shoe he takes. Can you imagine that? Like new, he says. Who the hell wants to wear somebody else's shoes?"

I drive down Cermak, the main drag of the old neighborhood, looking for Luka's butcher shop.

"Slow down," she says. "It's on this block. There. Park in front. Right here. Come in with me."

There is an old man ahead of us buying slab bacon and Polish sausage. He is talking with Luka the butcher in a language that sounds like Czech. My mother joins in, making some remark about Wisconsin and fish, and soon the three of them are talking and laughing. I hear her say to Luka something like, This is my son. He doesn't speak Czech. And Luka smiles, bows, and wipes his hand in his apron before shaking mine.

When the old man leaves, my mother continues the conversation, moving slowly along the meat case, pointing, questioning, buying Bohemian salami (*praski*), hot dogs, *jaternice*, and pork chops while the

butcher trims and weighs and wraps and marks each package. She mentions something about roast lamb, and the butcher is silent a moment, then motions for us to come behind the counter and follow him.

He grasps the large, stainless steel handle of the walk-in cooler and motions to step inside. The door clicks solidly shut behind us. It is cold enough inside to see our breath. A dozen lambs hang from the top hooks along one wall, while five or six suckling pigs hang here and there between sides of beef. There are rabbits, still in their fur, strung around the top of an old wooden barrel filled with fresh bones. And in the corner near the door, a large buck hangs from the ceiling by its antlers.

I lose the language entirely as mother and Luka begin to converse in a different tongue, possible Serbo-Croat. Though the langauge sounds harsh, their gestures are warm and benign. Luka, wrapping his arm around the deer, my mother rubbing her hand up and down the blue-white skin of a lamb, then lifting a rabbit's head, puckering her lips, murmuring baby sounds into the eyes, and blowing gently into its fur. Both Luka and she begin laughing, and Luka leads us out of the cooler with his bare arm gently around my mother's waist.

We follow him deeper into the store where an old man in a dirty white apron watches a lamb turning on a spit powered by an electric motor. In a pan on top a nearby oven lies the hind quarter of another roasted lamb. Luka tears a pieces of the greasy meat with his fingers and places it between my mother's lips.

"Mmmm," she says, turning to me. "This is delicious. They're all out of pig. I'll have Luka wrap up

THE GHOST OF SANDBURG'S PHIZZOG

the rest of this lamb to take home."

My father is waiting at the door. He meets my mother halfway, huffing up the front steps, her arms loaded with packages. "Leave the car in front," he tells me. "I'll put it in the garage later."

"Here," she says, handing him a shopping bag. "I got some roast lamb from the butcher. Put it in a large pan and put it in the oven right away. We'll have it for supper. And there's smoked fish we brought from Wisconsin, and all kinds of cheese."

"I've already got the pork loins in the oven," he pleads.

"Good. We'll have it for supper tomorrow."

"There's just never enough, never enough for you," he says.

"Did you put salt and caraway on the pork? I told you to sprinkle caraway. Leave the door open till he gets the suitcases in. Jesus, that's a long ride. I thought we'd never get home."

He has set the kitchen table for three, in anticipation of our arrival. He has cut the round loaf of Bohemian rye in half and then cut that half into thick slices, stacked neatly on a plate. Three gleaming pilsner glasses stand before each plate, with paper towels folded for napkins. A can of peas and a can of sauerkraut are on the counter near the sink, ready to be opened and emptied into waiting pots.

"Put that stuff in the icebox," says my mother, pulling a housedress over her head, knocking her wig askew. "This damn thing!" she flings the wig into an empty chair. My father looks at me and shakes his head. "I'll make the sauerkraut tomorrow when I make the dumplings," she says. "You've got this oven too damn high."

THIS HORSE OF A BODY OF MINE

"How was the car?" asks my father.

"Fine. You should have seen the clouds of black carbon that came pouring out," I tell him.

"It should run like new now," he says.

"Nobody drives cars like that anymore," she tells him, opening the oven door, testing the lamb with her fingers. "Get rid of that relic already."

She unwraps the oily newspaper on the center of the table, revealing a pile of smoked fish the color of old gold. "Look at these, aren't they beautiful?" she says.

"Yeah, but who's going to eat all this?" my father says. "You throw half of it away. Everything ends up in the alley."

Standing before her plate, she breaks the head off a smoked fish with one silent push of the fork, runs her red fingernail underneath and peels back the gold skin as if she were removing a glove. Inserting her fork in the pink-white meat of the back, she loosens entire chunks free of bones. "Wait till you taste this," she tells my father, buttering a slice of rye bread.

He opens three bottles of imported beer from the refrigerator and fills each glass.

"Sit down," she says. "The both of you. Cut some cheese. I'll make some coffee. Where's that bakery I bought?"

"I bought bakery this morning from Vesecky's," father says. "What did you go and buy bakery for?"

"I bought this up in Wisconsin. Some joint we stopped in. They don't know how to bake up there."

I move the smoked fish out of her way as she sets the pan of roast lamb on a hot plate, tosses the potholders in the sink, and closes the oven door. The

kitchen smells of roast pork, caraway, lamb, fish, rye bread, beer, and coffee perking.

"Now eat," she says.

The sins of my childhood were small and private. Most of my confessions were appetites: the taste of a candy bar in my closet before taking Holy Communion. My penance was prayer, which came easy. I sought, and now bestow forgiveness, in the same breath.

The lamb and fish and bread fall apart on my plate. I pick up a fork and taste the lamb, then butter a slab of rye with sweet butter, sprinkling it with salt. The taste of warm lamb and fresh rye in my mouth rekindles old desires. The response is instant: more. There is no time to talk, to think, to see anything but the table of food before me. "Here, try a hunk of this," says my mother with a full mouth, handing me a shank dripping with grease, dropping it on my plate. The fork suddenly seems foreign, in the way. I begin to eat with both hands, to rejoin the family in a ritual of consumption more embracing than the laws of etiquette. The cold glass of pilsner slides in the oil and grease of my fingertips, but I clutch it firmly, raising it to my lips the way a priest would cradle a chalice.

Then mother is pouring hot coffee and father is carrying boxes and bags of bakery from the pantry. "I've got a fruit coffeecake, cherry, pineapple, prune, and blueberry," he says. "And a poppyseed loaf and an almond twist. Which one should I open?"

"Open all of them," she says, breaking the string around the white boxes in both hands. "What's the difference? You can't save bakery, you know that."

THIS HORSE OF A BODY OF MINE

While she cuts the coffeecake, my father gathers the loose string, winding it around his hand, slipping it over the back doorknob where he keeps rubberbands.

At six the next morning I rise to drive to Wisconsin. I see mother in the light of the kitchen, her robe, her gray hair, saying the rosary at the table. She has a small statue of the Blessed Mother in front of her, along with a votive candle, an ashtray, her cigarettes and coffee.

I move quietly behind her, press my hands into her shoulders, bend down to kiss her on the cheek. "Don't bother with anything," I whisper. "I'm all right."

With the rosary wrapped in her fingers, she squeezes my hand, attempts to rise, and begins to say, "Don't forget..." in the midst of her prayers, while I press harder into her flesh for her to continue, to remain just where she is.

My father waits in the garage with the door open. He hands me a lunch bag mother has packed for me. "You want some shoes?" he says. "They're like new. Here, try these on. Wear something solid on your feet instead of those gym shoes. I had the shoemaker put new soles on this pair. Look at the beautiful job he did. That guy's an artist."

"They're a little too big," I tell him.

"Wear two pairs of socks," he says.

"My car looks great."

"I washed and Simonized it, took all the rust off the bumpers, cleaned the whole inside. Once you learn to take care of things, they'll last forever."

The Landscaper

He was no longer at home. That was the way Sandor Waterman saw it. Forty-nine years old, a reasonably successful landscape painter in his adopted Portal County, Wisconsin, he walked the edge of the lakeshore near his cabin studio that morning, studied the imperceptible lines that both distinguished sand, water, sky, yet made the composition whole, and thus framed the scene before his eyes as he had often done. Everything was here. It always was. Only the coming light would make a difference. And that seemed beyond him now.

That morning he returned to his cabin studio, made breakfast, then quietly proceeded to destroy all of his paintings that remained.

It was a question of diminishment. Not as large a talent as he once thought himself to be. Not as successful a painter as he set out to become twenty-five years ago. Not as dramatic a life as he expected to live. No revelations whatsoever in that no man's land of love, that space between his life and art.

Though he had traveled the country and the world, he had never really left home. The rural landscape satisfied some vague need of nature for a while, but now with his wife on her own, his children scattered, Sandor Waterman finished his last watercolor of the Nelson barn and apple orchard yesterday evening and now watched the fire curl the edges of the heavy paper and flow in.

He powdered the gracefully turned ash in his fingers — his future, his past, Sandor himself. A moderately successful Midwestern landscape painter coming to an end. Not distinct enough to be great, to be different, to be known anywhere else but here, where the tourists sought his work in the way of

expensive souvenirs, memories of weathered barns, stone fences, abandoned farms, quiet waters that all reflected the motto of Portal County: God's Country. Buying a Waterman painting to display in the living and rec-rooms of their suburban split-level homes in Milwaukee and Chicago, they felt they owned a piece of Portal County, claimed a part of the artist's vision as their own.

The same vision Waterman denied the morning he found himself out of place, determined to rid himself of the past. All the paintings. All the tools of his trade.

For Sandor Waterman's decision was to walk out of his life a failed painter, abandon the Portal County landscape in the dark, and find what there was to ordinary life in the time that remained.

Of the artists he knew personally in Portal County, of the lives of famous artists he had read about in books and magazine articles, none to his knowledge had ever quit. And that alone confirmed his action. The seriousness of his life's calling was considerably in doubt. Factory workers quit their jobs. Shoe salesmen, secretaries, short-order cooks. True artists remained artists all of their lives.

From the time of grade school it was evident that Sandor Waterman could draw. A born artist, some said. In his last year of high school he won a scholarship to art school in Chicago. When Portal County began to attract a steady stream of summer tourists in the 1950's, artists from the outside settled in, finding their work in demand, the quiet country scene financially lucrative. Sandor, after ten years of teaching, desiring release from the classroom and the city, was one of the them.

THE LANDSCAPER

His work, adequate at first, got increasingly better. What he learned in art school, what he studied, what he perfected, was technique. All kinds of ways to make the Portal County landscape as beautiful and real as it appeared in all seasons. He did not attempt to make it more so, however, to venture beyond the very reality he was witness to. To know the true color of the field that wasn't there. To lean the trees through line as subtle as a bird's ascent. To make the deserted farmhouse feel as empty as it was.

He familiarized himself with the particulars of the land, the water, the air that was Portal County. He knew that. He knew the plant-life in season, the subtle hues in the families of birds, the colors of ice, the movement of sun. Still, there was a way with it which made him feel alienated, even strange. Sometimes, studying the paintings of others, others who had also adopted the Portal County landscape, he felt one or two of them attempted a revelation of the land he never understood, but knew was there.

This depressed him. Led him to an increasing dependency upon straight bourbon and coffee laced with brandy. Darkened his perspective to see others reap mysteries from the landscape he could not envision.

And that, he suspected, was talent, or genius, or illumination bordering upon the divine.

While what Sandor Waterman rendered was technique. Perfection.

And knowing that most of the people who purchased paintings of Portal County could seldom distinguish the difference, made Sandor suicidal at times.

THE GHOST OF SANDBURG'S PHIZZOG

There came periods, under a clear night sky of no moon, when he would stand perfectly still in a field, staring into the stars until he fell.

A time came when he found himself manufacturing paintings of weathered barns in the landscape, though each was executed unmistakably in his customary precise style, because his wife's records revealed that weathered barns in Portal County sold extremely well.

The time came, near his decision to destroy everything, when most of his paintings were commissions, and he was relieved of even the choice of subject matter.

"Could you do a painting of our summer house?"

"I'm looking for someone to paint my boat under full sail in the bay, with the bluff, some pine trees, and a sunset."

"I have a photograph of my grandfather's old farm in Pennsylvania. Can you make a watercolor of it?"

Yes, said Sandor Waterman who at the peak of his career could paint anything. He had even amazed himself one time, a little too much brandy in his coffee all morning, when he knocked off an incredibly fine painting of the local Baptist church, his eyes closed all the while.

And all this disturbed him.

Though it did not disturb his wife, Joan, whom he had met in art school back in Chicago, and who looked upon his work as both beautiful and marketable. He gradually allowed everything to rest in her hands, appreciative of the freedom her actions provided for him to paint without interruption.

THE LANDSCAPER

The more successful he became, the less he was seen in the county. He no longer painted on location, relying on memory and slides. He answered no phones, no mail. The only approach to Sandor Waterman for the past 10 years was through the painter's wife who protected his privacy fiercely, and allowed few but the very wealthy customers near him. She acted with a certain flair, however, a genuine concern for her husband's time, and in this way was not entirely dismissed by prospective buyers and natives alike, though few of the local people thought much of her arty clothes and city ways.

She saved him, too, from the distraction of ordering and purchasing supplies, the matting and framing of his work, and all the bookkeeping. Sandor questioned his own heart at times, whether these actions on her part constituted love.

"A couple from Kenilworth called yesterday afternoon concerning a painting of a county courthouse in Illinois," she would approach him over the breakfast table. "It seems the husband's father was once a judge there. I told them to send a slide or Polaroid, and you would try to do the painting by Christmas."

And Waterman would nod his head, sipping hot, black coffee, his eyes closed, trying to calm the sharp pain lodged behind his eyes which he often awoke with in the grayness of early morning.

"You're drinking too much, don't you think? It's affecting your work. You're not painting as well, or certainly has much as last year. I'd like to know what' wrong. Tell me, once, what the hell is going on? Your color is off. Your lines tend toward the vague. In another month the season will be in full swing. The summer people will be here to see your

new work, and what will you have to show?"

Waterman concentrated on the word "new."

"You haven't painted the center of the county in some time," she said.

He got up and opened the cabinet above the sink, found the bottle of brandy, and poured it into the coffee mug.

"That's what I'm talking about. Why are you always depressed? Listen to me! Go out and paint today. It's beautiful. Perfect weather. Go out to the center. The Holstrum farm. Remember the Holstrum farm? The one with the windmill near the barn, and the morning glories trailing up? You haven't painted that in years. People will love it."

The center of Portal County retained an innocence, a privacy and purity of place that was off-the-beaten-track for tourists, and very special to Sandor Waterman. Portal County was slipping into sameness, a resort community that in time would be no different than any other resort area or suburban development. And how much was he, the artist, responsible? Was the sale of his art any different than the greed of developers subdividing large tracts of land into one-acre parcels for gentlemen farmers? The greed of the gift shop people, motel people, condominium investors? Sandor Waterman no longer painted the center because he wanted to preserve it from the hands of real estate people.

Joan was right. She knew the business, the history of the county, the history of Sandor Waterman. She loved what she could see. She loved Sandor Waterman for his ability to show exactly what was there. What she saw. No secrecy in either the setting or the artist. No self. His painting made things clear. And

THE LANDSCAPER

she loved him for this. She loved being able to tell prospective buyers exactly where a painting could be found in the Portal County landscape. Her life was that certain.

It was true Sandor Waterman had not painted the center for years. He had deliberately avoided it. Abandoned it. Kept a certain distance from the woman, Iris, the stone woman, a dancer, it was rumored, who occupied a summer residence there alone in the farmhouse rented from the widow of Carl Stoven.

They had discovered each other that first summer some five years ago when Sandor Waterman attempted to go into the center and begin painting. It was some distance from the last outbuilding, beneath a large maple tree, where he came across an intriguing arrangement of stones that spoke to him in the ancient ways of men who found a language to the earth.

The stones had been removed from one of the picturesque and slowly diminishing stone fences of Portal County that divided a field close by. They were smooth and white, pulled recently, it seemed to Waterman, from the very depth and center of the fence. He set up his campstool and materials, and prepared to work the stone arrangement into his painting of the Stoven barn.

"I would leave them alone," she said. "Even to paint them is to remove them, to take away their natural light. You can't imagine how they must speak with each season, or what they become in rain and under the full moon. Can you see them held within a shell of ice? How the sun must share their secrets." She came from somewhere behind him,

barefooted, dressed in a long, white muslin skirt and blue workshirt, her hair the color of the fields in late September.

Sandor's first impression: an overly sensitive woman, given to affectation. An art school type that he always avoided in favor of the practical virtues of Joan.

"You're afraid of me," she smiled.

No, Sandor shook his head.

"Come closer then. Here. Hold a stone in each hand. Know the surface, the center. Close your eyes. Feel them as the weight of seeds, the delicacy of eggs. Now move with them slowly, turn. Set them down, anywhere. Toss them. Wherever they are, they belong. Their art is precisely what calls you to their attention. Which is sufficient. No? The philosopher's stone. What do you know of *kare sansui*, the dry landscape, the sermons in stone?"

When he confessed that he did indeed fear her, she told him that was hopeful because without fear there was no understanding of the darkness. Soon after, they became lovers. Summer lovers. And much of his knowledge and fascination concerning the center revolved around Iris, though he knew little about her except that when he was with her, when they made love, when the stones were amidst them in the back fields, he was not Sandor Waterman, the popular landscape painter of Portal County. He was simply a man remembering the love of a woman whose very presence nurtured a desire for repose.

"The state magazine is sending someone here to interview you on Friday," said Joan. She sat across from him at the table, thumbing through a recent issue of the magazine. "I thought perhaps an hour

THE LANDSCAPER

after lunch would be perfect," she continued. "It's important we give them some time. They said they would bring a photographer along, and they are very interested in featuring one of your paintings for their fall cover. Do we have anything on hand that might work? Or maybe you could do something, you know, something real Portal County-ish before they arrive. Maybe that line of maples along County H. You could do that without thinking."

Sandor Waterman slowly turned his head, no. No more.

"It's important. Really it is. A lot of people see that magazine."

He filled his mug with brandy again and a splash of coffee.

"You're not going to be able to work," she said.

Sandor Waterman stretched and slowly turned his head from left to right, then began a circular motion, something the stone woman, Iris, had taught him to ease the tension in his neck and shoulders. He was going for a walk along the shore. He wasn't sure when he would be back.

"You're wasting time."

Without thinking he reached across the table and struck her.

"You bastard," she whispered, speaking through her fingers spread open across her mouth.

I'm sorry, he said, pushing her hand away, attempting to rub the pain from her face. I'm just very tired of all of this, of you. I'm tired of what you've done to me, unintentionally, and what I've allowed you to become through silent neglect. I do not have much to say, which I think, ideally, is a virtue. I am not who I thought I was, or where I hoped

to be. And this, really, has nothing to do with you except our life together is false, like most married lives, and I don't know what love is or where to look for it. But it's not here, and it's not us.

"Don't burden me with your own failures. I've given you my life."

I didn't ask for it.

"Merely being Sandor Waterman's wife was asking enough."

I asked nothing of you that you didn't take for yourself.

"You would be painting dairy signs on the sides of barns if it weren't for me. You would be nothing."

I'm aware of that.

"You'll end up another drunken local, a nobody, painting names on mailboxes."

No, I won't do that. I'll leave. As I want you to leave. Take whatever you need, whatever you want. The paintings are yours, whatever you can get for them. This place too.

"Keep the paintings. They're not all that good. You really don't have it in you to be great. Talk about false! Look at your own paintings."

I've known that for a long time.

"But they are the *last* of the Sandor Waterman's," she laughed. "And that will sell."

All that summer Sandor painted less than a dozen landscapes. He had the phone disconnected, refused to answer the door, allowed the mail to pile up, reading only the occasional postcard from his vagrant daughter, Adriane, somewhere in Tunisia: *Dear Pops, The desert here is filled with the kind of light that falls on Portal County in July. I miss the smell of rain. I've missed you most of my life. Where is mother? Come*

THE LANDSCAPER

see me. Love, your daughter, Adriane

He stood in the fields at night, stargazing. Slept in orchards under cherry and apple trees cradling the sky. Collected beach stones in the name and love of Iris. Wrapped his arms around tall, white birch trees, rubbing his face against the bark. And near the end, in those moments of morning and night upon the beach, sought the beginning and end of horizons.

It was all there, all here, almost within reach. But he was not in it.

Once, perhaps, as a child. When he dug holes in the back-yard, hoping to reach China. When he climbed trees to touch the blue of robins' eggs. When he changed the light of the sun into fire, using a small magnifying glass and paper. When he opened the door of the house to the year's first snow and stepped into the silent white streets before anyone else was up, before anyone knew.

He would like to be the field, the fencepost, the tree transformed by snow.

He would like to be the fish poised in the light of the water above, the light transfigured to ice in December.

He would like to be the rock on the road's edge, split by the green shoot of a wildflower in spring, whatever color it manifests — violet, for certain.

Sandor Waterman could not paint this.

In the waning nights of summer he read essays by Emerson, the Upanishads, and the Bhagavag Gita: *There is no existence for the unreal and the real can never be non-existent.* But he could not make the meaning understood in the movement of his own life.

In early fall he rid himself of what remained and prepared to leave.

THE GHOST OF SANDBURG'S PHIZZOG

The night of his departure from Portal County, he visited Iris for the last time. Beyond the burlap curtains of the windows, the stones resting on sills, he made love to her twice, pressing his hands into the solid soft whiteness of her shoulder flesh, feeling the emptiness of himself like an echo.

"You have no place now," she murmured. "Only the moist, soft spot of earth where the stone once lay. You are ending a composition."

Realizing it.

"And loving me makes no difference?"

None.

"Good. Perhaps you will find it all needs your attention."

Perhaps not.

"Yes. Even more difficult. But certain."

He kissed her eyelids shut and felt the shape of her eyes slipping beneath his lips. Felt her own lips open and the warmth of her breath.

She reached for a small, round stone beside a candle near her bed, rolled it in the darkness of her hand, held it like something alive in the hollow of her hand, then placed it in his, gathering his fingers over it in a loose fist.

"To live and love without knowing," she kissed him, he recalled, in the sign of the cross.

Leaving Portal County for Chicago, he noticed how the landscape changed in subtle ways at first, and then, nearing Milwaukee, how far the urban sprawl had spread. The stars were dulled by industrial smoke. The whole city seemed sequestered. While the sweet smell of earth behind him suddenly turned gritty and stale.

THE LANDSCAPER

Turning off the interstate, he plied the backroads in search of a farm he deemed the last Wisconsin outpost bordering his homestate of Illinois, finally parking next to the pasture of a woman he liked to be near, the lady of the lambs, and slept in his car.

He awoke to a morning not unlike Portal County, but for the sound of lambs, a cluster of black-faced, smoky-soft animals, and a woman in their midst, waving to him, her hair the same color as their wool in sunlight.

"I have a guest room, you know. I don't normally expect my friends to sleep outside. Except for strangers, of course, like you. Hell, I thought you were dead. Why didn't you call? I've written. Your phone is out of order or something. I've even thought of coming up to buy a new painting, if only I could be sure of dealing with you directly, bypassing that protective wife of yours. What is she afraid of? Does she think I'm going to steal you? Put you in my loving care? She's probably right!

"You've certainly taken on the role of the recluse since I saw you last." She brought her hand behind his head and kissed him gently on the brow. "You're a cold creature on the outside, but I understand your kind.

"Would you like to paint here today? We can have a picnic in the field later. Jesus, you look terrible. But you've come to the right place. I'll mix you a potion in my blender. Are you ill? You look absolutely white. Almost sick, I'd say. Hug me, Mister. Oh, you are *so* still! Barely a heart beat. How do you do that? Are you a yogi? Teach me to be still, Mister. Look at me. No, here, deep, deep into my eyes. I'd say it's a bad case of repressed desire. Hold my hand."

THE GHOST OF SANDBURG'S PHIZZOG

He walked with her among the lambs, delighting in her affection for animals, delighting in her head resting against his shoulder. Later in the afternoon, sitting beneath a tree, a picnic lunch spread out before them, Sandor attempted to show what had happened in his life, poking a stick at the weeds, upturning small stones. Some of the words came, but most of his feelings he found too illusive to define. He played with the stick in his hand till it settled comfortably between his fingers like a brush, and suddenly seeing his way, dropped it.

"Of course you're an artist! Why do you doubt it? I say you are. Everybody says you are. People care about your work. You are not just another Sunday painter. Your paintings add meaning to the lives of others. You may not see it or believe it, but it's true. On the walls of my house, your Portal County is important to my well being, don't you see? Don't tell me about feeling false. You're the only honest man I know."

Waterman remained silent. Watching the fence line, the barn, the trees, the fields change in the warming light.

"If you came to me for sympathy, you came to the wrong person. I don't know what goes on inside you artists, how it grows, how you keep it alive, why it dies. I just don't know how to treat it. The ego. Does that need continual nourishment? Animals have no ego. They're a lot easier to love than people. So what's to become of Sandor Waterman? Why do you make life so difficult for yourself? Leave it alone. Keep the bad stuff out of your system. Toxins in the body. Get rid of them."

Sandor moved to hold her, play his hands upon the

THE LANDSCAPER

wooliness of her hair, rub her eyes, her nose, her lips with fingers that seemed to be losing touch.

"I want you to be well," she told him. "Be well! Are you with me? Promise me, if you become ill, you will call me. You will come see me. Promise? I want you alive."

They talked and drank and hiked and ate and took comfort in the lambs all about them, carrying them in their arms, holding them in their laps. As darkness began to approach, Sandor held onto her till he was certain that what he held was the spirit, the murmuring spirit of all living things. He could feel her, the lambs, the grass, the trees, the earth, as part of his body.

He tried to explain to her that the silence she revered in him was already hers. That the stillness of the lamb became her. But she could not believe this nor touch his despair. And he could not tell her how much quiet sorrow he felt in all God's creatures, in all His goodness, including the goodness within her.

"There's such a restlessness inside of me, I could kill," she said.

Sandor held her head gently in both hands while darkness settled in and claimed all but the closeness of her body, which was now his, as he took her quivering breath into his own silence.

In the city of Chicago, where his grandmother once lived in a very old neighborhood, where he was born and raised but had mostly abandoned during his Portal County period, he drove immediately to the North Side, found a small, unfurnished studio apartment near Lincoln Park, and waited to see what he would do next.

He ate very little. He read the few books he had

brought with him. He sat on various park benches in the late afternoon, watching and listening to the people, the Blacks, the Hispanics, the Southern white, the young in their games. He did not venture to the lakeshore nor visit the Art Institute. At night, alone in the apartment, he played the radio but did not listen closely. He watched Sandor Waterman till sleep redeemed the day.

He began riding the bus downtown each morning. He mingled with the shoppers in Marshall Field's and Carson's but purchased nothing. He visited the public library and sat there just to be inside it once again. He walked Michigan Avenue and became an habitual benchsitter in Grant Park near the Art Institute, absorbed yet absent amidst all the clamor of the city, feeding the pigeons, reading old newspapers, dozing off along with the rest of the old people, the bag ladies, the dispossessed.

One day a "Clerk Wanted" sign appeared in the Michigan Avenue window of an Oriental Import Shop, and Sandor walked in to apply. His entrance was heralded by the sound of chimes in the dark, empty store. He closed the door behind him and waited for someone to appear. Tables and shelves were filled with Oriental vases, lamps, and carved figures. Tapestries hung from the walls along with silk paintings of mountains, mist and sea.

A gray-haired man dressed in a dark suit nodded to Sandor Waterman, and Sandor shook his hand, bowed his head slightly, and explained that he was interested in applying for the position of clerk. No, he told the Japanese gentleman, he had no experience in art or sales, but he had a good feeling for the shop and all the works of art on display. He

THE LANDSCAPER

often felt a sense of peace gazing into the windows as he walked by. And if the gentleman would be so kind as to give him a week's trial, Sandor Waterman would work without salary or commission. Mr. Tanaka smiled, agreed it would be fine, but insisted on paying Mr. Waterman a minimum salary for his first week.

Sandor, in his quiet approach to people, his tendency to listen, proved himself perfect for the position that first week, selling a five hundred-dollar hand-painted vase, a porcelain tea set, and a brass Buddha. It all came very natural to him. People said something was beautiful and Sandor agreed. When a problem or question arose which he felt unqualified to answer, he called upon Mr. Tanaka, who gladly assisted.

There was something whole and complete about the work. The objects in the shop lent to the aura of peace he felt. Customers were few, almost all of them buyers, and never too demanding. Mr. Tanaka was mostly in the back doing books, transacting business quietly over the phone. Sandor moved slowly down the narrow aisles, familiarizing himself with the pieces, inevitably discovering himself in the reflection and shadows of the front window display, his arms folded, looking out at the light on the street.

On his coffee breaks, he sat at the counter of a small restaurant across the street, listening to the people around him, the noises emanating from the kitchen. He rummaged through old copies of daily newspapers left on the counter, glancing at the photographs, studying the crosswords. The back pages were usually filled with either human interest photographs or sporting events. Faces held his attention.

THE GHOST OF SANDBURG'S PHIZZOG

"I can take better pictures than that," the waitress said. "How do you suppose you get a job like that, taking pictures for the newspapers? I've got a good eye for things, my teacher said. I'm taking a photography course at the 'Y'. Last term I took two courses in painting. Watercolors. You want some more coffee?"

Her name was Cindy Davinci, 19 years old, a high school dropout of unknown parentage, raised for a while as a foster child on a farm in southern Wisconsin. But drifting on her own now for the past few years. She lived alone in a basement apartment on the West Side of Chicago in a neighborhood once solidly Slavic but now changing. She lived for a year with a young man separated from his wife and three children, but on the day he was to appear in court for a hearing on child support he suddenly vanished. He left his portable TV and some shirts in the closet. When Sandor made love to her the first time on the torn sofa in her living room, he traced a sinuous, thin white line from her throat to her left breast. It seemed alive.

"Guess how I got that," she said. His eyes appeared to well and subside, then well again. He gently pressed her full lips together in his fingers as if he were sealing a wound. All night he slept with her head cradled in his arm, which was numb, useless, just hanging there when he awoke.

"Do you still pray?" she asked him, out of the blue.

And Sandor smiled and thought a long time. No one had ever asked him that before. The word "prayer" seemed foreign and unpronounceable. He was almost certain he hadn't uttered it since childhood.

Some weekends she spent at his apartment show-

THE LANDSCAPER

ing him her album of photographs, walking with him through Lincoln Park Zoo like father and daughter, hand-in-hand, buying ice cream, popcorn, and balloons, taking pictures of animals.

"You know, I never saw a zoo till I moved here a few years ago? And I've never even been to a circus. I saw a clown once in a Fourth of July parade back in Wisconsin when I was a kid, and he scared the hell out of me. Only one goddam clown in my whole life. But afterwards, when I thought about him, I loved him. I just love clowns."

The next weekend, when she arrived at his apartment late on Friday night, she opened the door and found the room dark. "Sandor?" she called. When she flicked the light switch on, she screamed. In the middle of the room knelt a clown, baggy coat, funny hat, white face, red rubber ball nose, painted red mouth curved down in sadness, and colored balloons floating above him, strung to the fingers of his prayerful hands. She thought she saw a smile on his real lips before she knelt down beside him, held him, cried, and then laughed.

She knew almost nothing about the man but still coaxed him to move in with her. She could pull none of his past from him except that he came from up north some time ago, knew Chicago, and would stay a while longer before traveling east or west, either direction suiting him fine. He knew something of the Japanese and the American Indian. But the revelations, which he sensed everywhere, even within her, were better left unsaid.

"Why all this goddam mystery?" she asked. "So what? Who cares? I really don't want to know," her voice rose in anger. "You're like a goddam rock!

Don't tell me anything. But tell me," and she began to laugh, catching herself. "Jesus, Sandor, I don't even know where the hell *I* came from!"

He looked at her watercolors tacked and taped to the walls of her kitchen, living room, bedroom and bathroom. They were crude, childish paintings of animals and flowers but vibrant in color and strangely arresting. One was a sheet, torn carelessly from a spiral drawing pad, almost equally divided in colors blue and gold.

"That's Wisconsin," she laughed. "My landscape. My abstract. I did it from memory. That's the view from my bedroom window, the hayfield in July when I was a kid. I'd wake up in the morning, and that's what I'd see. When I'd close my eyes at night, when I'd pray, I'd still see it. I'll see that damn place the rest of my life, I imagine. What about you, Sandor? What do you remember? What did you see as a kid? Why do I keep calling you Sandor? You're Sandy to me. Sandy, how do you like my art work?

"Oh, it's all such bullshit, isn't it?" she laughed. "Art, photography, who really gives a damn what you see, what someone else sees? I mean, it's there, right? Either you see it or you don't. You want to make someone's day? Give him a cup of fresh, hot coffee!" And Sandor began to laugh.

He followered her out to the backyard where they sat on a wooden bench beneath an apple tree, with the old Serbian landlady on one side of him and Cindy on the other. In a lingering October evening, the old woman peeled a bright yellow apple with a paring knife she kept in the pocket of her apron. She spoke no English, only cursed in a strange tongue when a stranger to the neighborhood walked down

THE LANDSCAPER

the alley and looked at the three of them on the bench.

As it began to get dark, the old lady wheezed a few times, picked away at a callus under her thumb, mumbled something and went into the house for the night.

Cindy leaned her head against the tree, her dark hair sticking to the bark, her eyes closed, her fingers turning small circles upon his hand.

Emerson entered Sandor's silence ... *a light shines through us upon things and makes us aware that we are nothing.*

He looked to the neighboring backyards filled with assorted refuse, broken light fixtures, old doors, abandoned cars. The bushes and trees that remained appeared to be starving or dead.

He brought his eyes to rest in the nightfall of the landlady's backyard, the marigolds, the mums, the white roses that hovered in a horizon he knew to be the newly painted back fence.

In the light that was left he stood before the landlady's small pond rimmed with flat stones, saw a reflection of the fruit and branches of the apple tree behind him extend from his own body, witnessed a single burnished leaf fall and dissolve him, heavenward, surging into a radiance of night.

Stars

Wherever I am in the world, whenever I think of my old neighborhood, I view the setting in miniature the way a child creates imaginary places. These are the boundaries, we would say in our hide-and-seek games. Or, these are the sidewalks here, I might say to myself alone. Streets here, alleys over here. Pretend these are lamp posts. And these houses, and people going up and down the street. A church, a school, and over here a prairie. And a swamp. A train goes through here. And over there, way over there are some factories — No Man's Land.

All of this is still there.

Whenever I find myself outside my father's house, I view the houses of my friends, Davey Nactman, Joe Krachi, Billy Nolan, Johnny Hookstra, who lived in brick bungalows, two-story flats, basement apartments, and recall the games of war we played then: the Americans against the Germans and Japs; the card games of war on rainy days; the capturing of prisoners; the killing of the enemy. Innocence was not a word we used or understood, given our age — grammar school kids, public and parochial — and we switched with ease from good guys to bad guys many times within a day's play. My arms outstretched, engine screaming, machine gun blazing, I was often engaged in dizzying dogfights, my Messerschmitt crashing in flames, only to be resurrected moments later, aviator's helmet and goggles and my father's white silk scarf which I always snitched from his bottom dresser drawer, flying my Grumman Hellcat, shooting down Hookstra and Krachi in their Japanese Zeros, hightailing it back with Nolan (suffering a slightly damaged wing), guiding him home to safety under a rousing chorus of "Off we go, into the wild blue yonder!"

THE GHOST OF SANDBURG'S PHIZZOG

Davey Nactman seldom played these games with us, even if I promised to play whatever he wanted to play after we played war. He was always the first to get hurt and then quickly lost interest. He always had homework to do, music lessons, and listened to his parents who often cautioned him of the danger in our play. Once, in our tank battles, Davey was my driver. We lined up our forces (wagons modified to carry sawhorses in front for battering, large cardboard boxes to house the driver, cans of water for gas, piles of sand and stone for ammunition) at each end of the alley for boundaries, and on signal pushed the tanks as fast as we could run toward each other. Sometimes wagons would tip or fall over, and the cans of water spill on the driver, signifying immediate death. Davey, in our battle with Hookstra's Panzers, hit his head so hard on the concrete, he seemed stunned for a moment and then ran home screaming. Hookstra played for blood and tears. To just get wet was not dead enough for him. If you cried or ran he would come after you, hurling sand, stone, demanding you shout out the ultimate: "I surrender!" or "I'm dead!" He did not play with us often because he lived beyond our block. But when he did, his presence promised excitement, new boundaries, new games. He could make things up right on the spot. We were all a little afraid of him, but just being near him, or to have him on your side, gave added strength.

"Say, 'I'm dead!, I'm dead!'" he shouted after Davey, chasing him down the alley and through my backyard. But Davey refused to give in. "Crybaby!" Hookstra taunted him once Davey was safely across the street and on his front steps. "You little pimp!"

STARS

In Hookstra's mind the game was not over, and he adamantly proclaimed that Davey did not play fair, which was a serious charge we accused each other of often enough in our games. That and being a bad loser. To be a good loser was something like being called a nice boy. Victory was pure excitement and beyond judgment.

Krachi didn't give a damn one way or another. He had already forgotten tanks and wanted to play paratroopers on his front porch, since his brother Bobby had just finished jump school and was awaiting orders to go overseas. Nolan just laughed at everything and thought it was hilarious to watch Hookstra get mad.

Later that afternoon Krachi and I were jumping from his front porch, and Nolan and Hookstra were hiding behind bushes waiting to attack when Davey Nactman's mother came from across the street and told us Davey had a small concussion but would be okay. We shouldn't play so rough, she cautioned us. We shouldn't play games where we might seriously hurt one another. We were all welcome to play Monopoly or Sorry or cards at Davey's house. Or Mr. Nactman would be happy to teach us chess.

Though I was the only one who went to Davey's, and though I think now Davey may have been my best friend, going to his place to play games, staying inside, did not seem as much fun at the time as riding the elevated train downtown to the Chicago Loop on Saturdays with the other guys. Nolan's old man, a conductor, would let us stand outside on the noisy platform between the coaches, against the gates, and when the El began to rise from the groundlevel of our neighborhood, over and beyond the prairie and

factories of No Man's Land, we would watch everything diminish in size behind us and pretend to be taking off on a mission over Germany or Japan in our B-17 bombers. I would be dressed in my leather aviator's helmet and goggles, my father's white silk scarf, and my sheepskin flight jacket with my army air corps shoulder patch of gold wings on a field of blue with a white star and red center that my mother had sewn on. And together, Nolan, Krachi, Hookstra and I, would prepare to drop bombs over Germany, looking down and back upon our world, seeing it differently, subject to our command. I held sharply pointed bullet heads that my mother brought home from the war factory where she worked in No Man's Land. And I hollered "Bombs away!" when the train reached it highest altitude over Douglas Park, while Nolan, Krachi, and Hookstra made explosive sounds, as they peered down into the flame and smoke and destruction yelling, "Bull's eye! Bull's eye!" We would never get off the El downtown, but continually ride the Loop back and forth, stay on the same train with Nolan's old man for hours, finally getting off with him at our station when he was through working, or when we had tired of the game and wanted to play something else or see a movie.

There were solitary games as well, less combative, never shared with friends. Games of an only child whose parents both worked and left him with much time to himself. Home alone, afraid of the dark, I would turn on every light in the house and play priest, fashioning a chasuble of two dish towels pinned over my front and back, setting the kitchen table as my altar with a breadbox tabernacle and a

STARS

Pilsner glass as a chalice, genuflecting, mumbling my altar-boy Latin, offering body and blood to a small crucifix of palms my mother had tacked to the wall above the table. I wished for candles, but there were none. If I could have explained this all to Davey, in my manhood, if I could have understood it myself then, he might have known my aspirations were holy: service to the Word, as we were taught in school, but which was as much a mystery to us then as a God divided in three parts, Father, Son and Holy Ghost.

On rainy days, I would go up to the attic alone and play with a toy village that somehow came into our family from some relation in Europe. I would find the box my father had stored with the Christmas decorations, untie it, and carefully unwrap each handmade piece. Tiny wooden houses and shops, trees, fences, lampposts, horse-pulled wagons, a train with a gate and railroad crossing sign, people and farm animals. At Christmas, I would set the village under the tree along with a crib—the stable, the wise men, the star of Bethlehem — all within the circle of my electric freight train, and at night, under only colored lights and engine headlamp, gaze at a place so peaceful I wanted to live there.

A grown man, I wander everywhere these days in search of the village, the small town, the neighborhood, imagining life on the scale I lived as a child. My father, who waits for my return, who cannot sleep nights since the new, sodium street lamps were installed in streets and alleys as a measure of crime prevention, so that nowhere is even the inside of the house dark enough for him anymore, my father sits in the vague darkness of the kitchen and says I'm like a wandering Jew.

THE GHOST OF SANDBURG'S PHIZZOG

Davey Nactman got along well by himself. I was the one always standing on the sidewalk outside his place, calling him to come out and play. I was the one wanting to include him in our war games. I was the one, alone, imagining rituals, inhabiting tiny villages, making puppets to talk to, the one who inevitably found the interior of the house--basement, main floor, attic--too dark, too empty, and, in such a state of mind, felt only Davey understood the conditions and private rewards of solitary play.

"David hasn't finished his homework," said Mrs. Nactman. "But please come inside and wait. His father will be home soon. He can teach you some chess."

We all lived close to one another except for Hookstra who lived a few blocks north of us near the Dutch church and school he attended. Krachi lived next to me. Our backyards were separated by a brick fence his father, a mason, built from various common and face brick he had accumulated from the jobs he worked. Their backyard was filled with hills of sand and gravel, wheelbarrows, mortar tubs, stacks of new and old lumber, scaffolds, platforms, sawhorses and cement mixers. There was not one blade of grass or a single tree. The entire yard was paved, little by little, with concrete left over from jobs. It was one of our favorite playgrounds. There were materials enough to make war or build houses, cities, bridges, ships and planes. One day we converted a huge sand pile into an amusement park — roller coasters, water rides, a tunnel of love, and a parachute jump, all modeled after Riverview Park on the North Side of Chicago, a place some of us had visited only once.

STARS

Nolan lived with his father and two older sisters in a basement apartment across the street, a few doors away from Davey. There was another sister, a nun, who was a missionary somewhere in Africa. His mother was dead, and the two sisters took care of him and Mr. Nolan, who was a bald-headed, kind man who loved to laugh, spoke with a brogue, and always saw to it that "his boys" rode the El downtown with him, free, on Saturdays.

Krachi, Nolan, and I belonged to the same parish and went to the Infant of Prague grammar school. Hookstra attended the Dutch Christian school. And Davey went to the public school, which we all rather looked down upon. There were many arguments about which school was harder, public or parochial, and it was generally understood, especially among the Catholic parents, that their children were at least a year ahead of public school students the same age, and that the important thing about a Catholic education was discipline. We were supposedly better behaved because both priests and nuns routinely punished us for not following the rules. We had no idea what went on in Hookstra's school because Hookstra seldom spoke of it. Davey, however, did more homework than the rest of us, had his own card to the Chicago Public Library downtown, where we imagined his father sometimes took him on Saturdays, and received the best grades. That, too, made him less than one of us, in Hookstra's mind.

"Davey's got to do his homework," Hookstra would say if Davey could not join us in war or a game of hide-and-seek after supper, before the street lights went on.

"Davey's Mommy is calling home. Davey's got to

go home and practice the piano," he would tease, and push and poke till Davey inevitably yelled, "That hurts!" and begin to cry.

"See? A crybaby. Go home and let Mommy wipe your tears."

"Bully," Davey would holler, his voice choking, his face red.

"Hey, your Mommy teach you that? Huh? You twerp."

Since both my parents worked, I was given my own key to the house from the time I started grammar school. I would walk home for lunch, eat the sandwich my mother had left me in the refrigerator, then set the table for supper, when my father returned home from work. He left early every morning on the El for the city while I was still sleeping. My mother usually returned from her job at the factories after I left for school. Her hours were very irregular. Sometimes she would be sleeping when I came home for lunch. Often, she would work overtime, or be gone on another job, and I rarely saw her at all except for weekends. She worked what she called the graveyard shift, walking to and from the factories in No Man's Land. It was wartime, and they were geared for 24 hour production. Black smoke streamed from the tall stacks, depositing layers of soot on the white painted windowsills of the well-kept neighborhood. The women were always complaining how dirty everything was, the windows, the stairs, especially the white laundry strung out on the backyard clotheslines. There was one factory there that was supposedly an underground torpedoe plant with a single railway track that moved the torpedoes out at night. I would ask my mother if

she ever saw any torpedoes, but she would just close her eyes and shake her head. She kept her work at the war plant secret except for occasional surprises she would bring home, like a bullet head fashioned into a key chain with my name on it. I asked her to get one for each of my friends. Only Davey kept his polished in a box on his desk along with a collection of marbles and seashells.

Our mothers and fathers knew the parents of our friends mainly through the stories we passed on about them. I might say how Nolan's dad bought us candy at the El station before we rode downtown with him. Or how Mrs. Nactman always gave us something to eat when I went there, and Mr. Nactman was teaching me chess. Mrs. Hookstra never let us inside the house and always talked through a window or door partway opened. Mr. Hookstra was a scavanger who owned three garbage trucks and worked throughout the night. We never saw him at all.

My mother would speak Czech to Krachi's mother across the brick fence. She was a heavy woman who walked with a cane, always wore a housedress, and looked as old as my grandmother. She worried all the time. She spoke of Joey, my friend, as her baby, her change-of-life child, and was worried that someday he too might have to go to war. She could not mention Bobby, the oldest son, the paratrooper, without crying and feared he might be killed in the war. Old man Krachi, the stone mason, was seldom seen around the house. But on weekends, and late at night, he would sit in his undershirt on the backporch with a quart of beer at his feet, close his eyes, and fill the yard with sad, Slavic music on

THE GHOST OF SANDBURG'S PHIZZOG

his buttonbox concertina. In the kitchen, my mother's voice would softly accompany him, singing to herself in Czech, her eyes welling. If I were up late at night in summer, I would sit outside on the back steps in the dark, watch the stars, track the green light of fireflies, and listen to old man Krachi play the concertina till I could no longer keep my eyes open.

Davey Nactman's father and mine rode the same El together to work each morning, but neither man spoke to the other. Davey's father worked in some clothing business downtown and was studying law. My father was an accounting clerk. They were both quiet, private men who habitually read their morning and afternoon newspapers on the train. They wore dark suits, white shirts, ties, overcoats, and fedoras. Their shoes were highly polished. Each man walked his side of the street to and from work, leaving together about the same time each morning, but Mr. Nactman came home an hour or so earlier. Each man returned from the El station with his newspaper folded under his arm. My father, who was older, walked briskly with the rim of his fedora turned up, while Davey's father moved in slow, thoughtful steps, the brim of his fedora turned down, the hat sitting handsomely upon his head. His hair was as black as the soot that set on our window sills from the factories. There was always a heavy shadow of beard upon his face. He wore round, wire-rimmed glasses whenever he read. One day, as if a hand reached down and removed the figure from the setting, Mr. Nactman disappeared into World War II, leaving my father, who was declared 4-F, to walk the few blocks to the El and back alone, occasionally glancing at the shadows of the trees upon the empty sidewalk across the street.

STARS

Our heroes were Krachi's brother, the paratrooper, and Mrs. Sokup's son, Peppy, a nose gunner, who lived three doors north of my house. When Peppy came home on his first furlough, we would follow him down the block asking him what it was like to sit in the front of a plane like that, and how many planes he had shot down. After he left, Krachi and I would wait with Mrs. Sokup on the peeling wooden steps of her front porch for the mailman to see if there were any air letters from Peppy. She would hold the thin pages in her hand, trying to make sense of the empty spaces where the words had been cut out. In the center window of her house, she hung a small banner, red and white borders with gold fringe at the bottom and a blue star in the middle. Later in the war she opened a small box and showed us Peppy's Purple Heart. Weeks afterwards, the blue star turned to gold.

One Sunday on the corner of the block some of the men gathered with shovels, hammers and saws, and began building a war memorial in honor of the men in the neighborhood, living and dead, who fought for their country. They turned over the grass in the small, triangular space where the corner sidewalks crossed bordering the street, and erected a white picket fence, a flagpole, and a scroll of honor listing the names of all the serviceman. Old man Krachi was in charge of the construction, and with 2 by 4's, tar paper, and wooden stakes, formed a large star at the base of the flagpole which he filled with fresh concrete mixed by hand in a wheelbarrow. Throughout the afternoon, periodically, he could be seen on his knees before the star, tamping it to bring the water to the surface, smoothing it in gentle arcs with a

glistening trowel. The women came and planted red, white, and blue petunias along the borders. Then Mr. Herdlica, the air raid warden, brought an American flag and raised it slowly in ceremony while we sang The Star-Spangled Banner, the men and women with their hands over their hearts, the kids standing at attention, their arms angled in sharp salutes. After the dedication, old man Krachi sent Johnny back to the house for the concertina and some beer. For the remainder of the afternoon he sat on a small bench and played all the Bohemian songs I had heard at our weddings and anniversaries. Neighbors came and went all afternoon, including my mother and father and Mrs. Krachi. Davey and his father passed by across the street and waved. People sat on their front porches listening to the music well into evening. Old man Krachi trowled the cement smooth one last time as it began to grow dark, then from a paper bag in his tool chest, he scattered what looked like diamond dust on top of the wet star. Well after the street lights glowed up and down the block like low, full moons, he filled his wheelbarrow with shovels, tools, and concertina case, pushing it home down the walk, past people sitting on their front porches, nodding thanks, offering him beer, wishing him *dobrou noc* (good night) in the dark.

    The next morning before school Krachi and I stopped at the war memorial on our bikes. "It looks dry," he said. We touched the hardened star which had turned from gray to white. "Yeah, it's set," he said, pulling up the stakes, kicking away the forms and tossing the lumber into a pile. I rubbed my fingers over each point of the star. Later at morning

STARS

Mass, some of the sparkle dust remained on my prayerful poised hands.

Davey's mother was the youngest mother of all my friends. She never wore house dresses or aprons. Her hair was brown and long, her eyes like wet black olives, deeply set, her skin like a rich summer tan. Her voice always came as a surprise, it was so deep. There was a tremor to her laughter, a resonance. She was the most beautiful mother I had ever seen.

Their apartment did not smell of cooking like most of our houses. It smelled of perfume and flowers and Mr. Nactman's pipe smoke. There were paintings on the wall, a strange shaped candelabra on the mantle, a chess board inlaid on a small table with two red mahogany chairs, bookcases, and a baby grand piano in the living room. I was always happy to be invited in.

Sometimes I would just sit on the sofa and wait for Davey to finish practicing the piano. Sometimes Mrs. Nactman would sit beside him on the bench, gently place her fingers on the keys, and make music so slowly, so beautifully that the look on her face would change, and I felt different watching her. Davey would fold his hands in his lap and watch her fingers move over the keys. How did she make music like that? And how did the music make her face, already beautiful, turn into something even more beautiful and strange as she gazed into the ceiling, closed her eyes, and opened her lips as if she were lost in sleep? The first time I saw this I was frightened. It resembled a crazy woman on the next block who stared at the sky. I thought Mrs. Nactman had turned into a different person. But then she would finish playing, laugh in that low voice of hers, clasp

THE GHOST OF SANDBURG'S PHIZZOG

Davey's hand, sometimes kiss him on the cheek, and suddenly be herself again almost as if she had returned from some other place, the same way I would play war or priest, and then be called to come and eat, and I would sit down at the kitchen table and try to remember my surroundings and who I was.

My grandmother still lived in the city, the old neighborhood, and often on Sunday my father and I would drive there early in the morning to pick her up and bring her to our house for the day. While we went to church, grandma would prepare dinner, filling the entire house with smells of tripe soup, chicken paprika, bakery and rye bread. The heat of the kitchen would sometimes drive her to the backyard, wiping beads of sweat from her forehead into her apron, kneeling in the victory garden or the flower bed, carrying on a long conversation in Czech with Mr. and Mrs. Krachi. When we sat down to dinner, grandma would explain her conversation with the Krachis to mother, and my mother would interject English here and there for the benefit of my father and me. "They were talking about the old country again," my mother would say. "Nobody has heard anything from the relatives. Mrs. Krachi is worried her brother might be dead. She's afraid Bobby will be sent to Germany and be killed. She can't understand how he can jump out of a plane and be alive. It scares her to death. Parachutes."

One Sunday afternoon when Davey and I were playing on the brick fence, balancing ourselves to see who would fall first, either into the rose bushes in my yard, or the junk and concrete pavement in Krachi's, an old woman came down the gangway calling for Davey to come home for supper. My mother and

father had gone to visit a man my father worked with who had just lost a son in the war. Grandma was asleep in a chair in the yard when the old woman opened the gate and called again for Davey. Suddenly my grandma awoke, the two women looked shocked, and the two of them began talking in Czech. "That's my grandma Fischl," Davey said.

When Davey and his grandmother left, my grandma attempted to tell me in Czech, of which I understood very little, and broken English, how she knew Davey's grandmother from the time in Michigan where my grandparents once owned a farm. Davey's grandparents vacationed in St. Joseph and Union Pier ... the House of David, she laughed, grabbing my hair, trying to describe to men how the men there dressed in long coats and had long beards and wore their hair funny. *"Divati, divati,"* (look, look) she laughed, pulling my hair. Then she continued talking in Czech and made an angry face, and I lost her meaning entirely.

But I felt closer to Dave then. I liked him more than any of my other friends, though neither of us ever mentioned the incident, and I never saw his grandmother again.

Later, when my parents returned, the whole incident was retold at the supper table and more of the details of grandma's story were made clear, including the fact that Davey's grandparents occasionally bought eggs from my grandma and they would always argue over the price. A *žid*, my grandma called her.

Mother then recalled how just a few months ago Mrs. Nactman had come to get Davey. He and I were building model airplanes in the basement while

she was washing clothes. When Mrs. Nactman knocked, she opened the basement door to let her in, and while they were talking my mother began to apologize for the mess in the basement, including stacks and stacks of newspapers my father was saving for the sheenie who came down the alleys with his horse and wagon. My grandmother began laughing. My father merely shook his head with a slight smile. My mother said she felt so embarrassed. She hadn't realized what she said. To this day she can hardly face Mrs. Nactman on the street.

My father was always saving things for "the sheenie." I was at an age when I was trying to disassociate myself from all things foreign, especially the language of my mother and grandmother. I was an American, not a Bohunk or a Slovak or a greenhorn. "Sheenie," I suspected, was another Czech term for junkman. I kept my grandma a secret, out of the way from my friends who might label me a greenhorn too. I seldom mentioned her, and by refusing to use the little language I knew as a small child, gradually lost whatever meaning it once held for me.

At odd times during the week, especially on Saturdays in summer, I heard the call, "Raggggggggga a lionnnnnnnnnn, Raggggggggggga a lionnnnnnnnnn!" and the junkman appeared in the alley with his horse clopping on the cement pavement, and the green wooden wagon with large, red spoked wheels vibrating with old bed springs, piles of rusty scrap iron, and stacks of old newspapers. He was dressed in torn trousers, an old suit coat, and ugly, black shoes. Perched high on a bench, he held leather reins in one hand and a whip in the other, announcing his

presence in a cry, part call, part song, making clicking sounds in his mouth which the horse understood. He wore a soiled cap low on his forehead and a dirty pair of canvas gloves cut off at the knuckles. A stubble of gray beard covered much of his face.

Sometimes his approach was almost mysterious. My mother would look out the back kitchen window, and he would be sitting there with his horse and wagon, waiting. "The sheenie's here!" my mother would call out to my father, who would move quickly through the house, down the basement steps, and begin carrying bundles of neatly tied newspapers into the alley, occasional buckets of scrap metal. When he saw my father coming, the junkman would climb down from his bench, attach a feed bag to the horse's mouth, then walk to the back of the wagon and hang up a scale. Hardly any words were said, the rituals had been so well established. My father would ask him what he was paying for old paper and scrap iron this week, and the junkman would mumble a price, and my father would either accept it or say another figure, gaining perhaps an additional penny or two a pound, unless the junkman shrugged his shoulders or shook his head no. He picked coins out of a small leather purse, one at a time, and handed them to my father. The junkman never smiled. Never said thank you. Never said hello. Never said goodbye. My father, who preferred quiet acts of accomplishment to conversation, looked forward to his encounters with the junkman.

I witnessed almost every transaction, the comings and goings and dealings with the junkman, helped carry the bundles of paper to the wagon, yet kept my distance from him. I would ask about the horse's

name and inevitably receive some unintelligible reply which I pretended to understand. I had been raised, like all the neighborhood kids, to be wary of peddlers, gypsies, and coal men. Yet their sudden appearance, like the junkman's, lent an aura of mystery and excitement to the neighborhood. Milk men, ice men, knife sharpeners, fruit and vegetable peddlers were all a momentary celebration in the monotony of our daily routines, even our games. Very likely we would "play" one of them tomorrow, though the war elicited most of our passions for the time being, and though I never recall any of us "playing" the junkman since his figure seemed more comic than heroic, except for his horse which held us in awe.

While the junkman shifted the stacks of paper from the scale to the back of the wagon, I patted the flanks of the horse, felt the ripples in the sweaty skin, jumped backwards, startled, at the twitching of the flesh, the swaying of the head, the swish of the tail. Back on his bench, his body hunched, the reins in hand, the junkman yanked, made a clucking sound twice, and the horse began to move them slowly down the alley. I would watch and wait to hear his call once, twice, three times more in the distance till he turned near the El tracks and disappeared from sight. I never knew where he came from or where he went, or whatever became of him and all the pedlers after the war, when everything ended, everything changed.

After the junkman disappeared from view, I went down to the basement and my father handed me some coins. "Save it," he said, "so you have something when you grow older."

STARS

I was anxious to visit Davey after supper, the afternoon his grandmother met mine. I felt certain, now, I was almost a member of the family. Davey's grandmother had already returned home, as had mine. "Well, I heard your grandmother and Davey's had a nice visit," Mrs. Nactman said. "Please tell your parents to thank her for the bakery she sent back with my mother. It was delicious."

Mr. Nactman and Davey were seated at the chess table. "Sit down," Mr. Nactman said. "I'll teach you the game. Then you and David can play."

He explained how one side was black and the other white, named each of the carved pieces and showed me their moves. We have a bishop in church, I said. And Mr. Nactman smiled and said yes. The knight seemed the most complicated of all the chessman, but I liked it better than the king or the castle because it looked and felt like a horse. The game seemed less exciting than checkers and took longer to play, but I learned it well enough for Davey's sake, though I never mastered it or continued the game later in life. Davey almost always won. Checkers was still my choice, faster and more fun. When you captured a man in chess, you just quietly slid by and removed him. In checkers you could jump once, twice, three times, grab the men, keep count, make your own kings, and know immediately whether you were winning or losing. It all took forever in chess. And the process of victory, check and checkmate, was such a quiet victory you were hardly aware you won. "It's over," was all Mr. Nactman said when he checkmated Davey's white king. "The game is not on the board," he advised the two of us. "It's beyond the square. It's what you don't see but is there. Intangible evidence."

THE GHOST OF SANDBURG'S PHIZZOG

That night there was a practice blackout. I lay in bed hearing sirens, seeing planes fly low through the star-lit neighborhood skies, bombs dropping, the church, the schools, the factories, the El station all in flames, smoke billowing into clouds. I could see my mother standing in the dark in the war plant, bullets exploding all around her, but she untouched. Our fighters would be in the air then. On the ground we would spot the enemy planes through the smoke with giant searchlights, and our artillery guns and fighting planes would send the enemy crashing to defeat.

The wall above my bed was covered with crude, thumb-tacked drawings in pencil and crayon showing our planes in enemy dogfights, their wings, tails, and fuselages emblazoned with red suns, black swastikas, and blue stars. The stars, always imperfect, were the most difficult to draw until one day a school friend showed me how to make them by drawing one triangle upside down over the other. Jewish stars, an uncle of mine once called them. On my dresser were all the model airplanes I had built and a small statue of the Blessed Mother that glowed green in the dark for a while and gradually died till it resembled a piece of soap in daylight. I prayed to her that night that we would win the war, as the nuns and priests taught us to pray at school. So we would not be persecuted the way Catholics were in other parts of the world, at different times in history. Priests hanging from lamp posts, as one nun described it. People burned at the stake like Joan of Arc. Would we, as Catholics, have the strength of martyrs? The courage to suffer and die for our beliefs? *I believe in one God, the Father almighty, Maker of heaven and earth, and of all things visible and invisible ...*

STARS

Footsteps on the sidewalk, sirens unwinding, Mr. Herdlicka, the block captain's voice joined by other voices and a man's laughter. A flashlight in the gangway rippling the venetian blinds in my bedroom window. I find my father sitting alone in the dark kitchen lit only by the radio dial. "It's over," he said.

The street lights went on. Neighbors began gathering outside their houses in small groups. Up and down the block lights in the living room began burning one after another. Trains from the factories began rumbling, whistles and wheels screeching. Fire in the foundries blossomed, and the blue welding light in some factories began flashing in thousands of tiny, frosted glass windowpanes. An automobile started and moved through gears down the street. The gate man in his shack by the El station began ringing the bell, pushing the tall levers to lower the black and white crossing gates, waiting for the El train, the windows all lit, to pass by, sparks and blue flashes rolling out of the iron wheels. Old man Krachi took up his concertina. The neighborhood fell in place again.

In the morning when I awoke, two beautiful white lampshades floated above the Czech crystal lamps on each endtable beside the sofa in the living room. Some woman from the factory had made them for my mother. "They're parachute silk," she told me. "Black market. Don't tell anyone. I have something else for you. A surprise. Just wait. One of these nights, you'll see."

It was Hookstra's idea. Friday, after supper, we would capture Davey on his way home from piano lessons. We would blindfold him, take him prisoner.

THE GHOST OF SANDBURG'S PHIZZOG

And we would not let him know who we were. That was important. Absolute silence. We could not give ourselves away. Nolan said he couldn't play because his father was taking him to some church to hear a missionary priest talk about Africa. So that left Hookstra, Krachi, and me.

We waited in the alley, a block before his house, where we knew he would pass by alone. Krachi was lookout and signaled he was coming. We hid behind some garbage cans Hookstra had rummaged and come up with a man's old, black fedora. We waited till he almost crossed the alley, then grabbed him from behind while Hookstra pulled the hat tight over Davey's head, twisted his arm behind his back, and began marching him down the alley, signaling for us to follow. Davey immediately began screaming, figured it was Hookstra, called him a bully who picked on innocent people, screamed even louder as Hookstra twisted his arm tighter and brought his other arm around Davey's face, gagging his mouth. When, desperately, Davey gasped, "I can't breathe! I can't breathe!" Hookstra slowly released the gag but kept the pressure on Davey's arm just enough so that Davey understood he was to keep walking, stop screaming, Hookstra in step right behind him, leading him with his left hand on the back of Davey's shoulder, pressuring him when to turn and when to walk straight. We followed in step alongside and behind Hookstra, keeping the commandment of silence, occasionally testing one another, making faces to see if we could make the other guy laugh and give himself away, though Hookstra would lunge after us with a kick, show a stern face, make us believe this was a serious mission, taking a prisoner.

STARS

The neighborhood alleys all ran north and south, though as you approached a major east-west throughway, alleys paralleled it on both sides, creating this grid of interconnecting passage ways. If you knew the neighborhood, the secrecy of our alley playgrounds, you could go anywhere, from one neighborhood to the next, and even beyond.

We were already outside our territory, and I sensed this immediately, this feeling of being out of place, though a relative sameness and security existed in the painted fences and garages, gardens and well-kept backyards. The few people who saw us either smiled at our games, or told us to go play in our own neighborhoods.

It was that time of the evening before dark when kids got in their last mad rush of play — "It" or "Hide-And-Go-Seek" — knowing that twilight was brief, and the streetlights soon would go on and we would be called home to bed. There was an urgency, then, that we finish our capture of Davey before dark.

Hookstra suddenly turned, motioned with his head to come closer, and whispered "The swamp" in our ears.

We came to the east end of an alley which abutted a major north-south street which marked not only our neighborhood boundary, but the end of alleys, the beginning of No Man's Land and the city itself, where we rarely ventured on foot or bike except to gradually ascend and soar above it on Saturday El rides, or drive into it in our fathers' automobiles. The lines of demarcation were not that distinct, but the buildings were different and began to take on more massive shapes. There were fewer houses, flowers

and trees. Fewer people. It was dirtier, noisier. There were more trucks and railroad tracks. Sidewalks disappeared. Pavements were cracked, curbs broken. The streets were made of large bricks. In the distance you could see the tall buildings of the city. In the foreground, though, just after crossing the busy street, were some coalyards, small businesses and warehouses, and squares of open prairies in between bordered by the factories and war plants on the other side, a perimeter of smokestacks and railroad crossings that one way or another those outside had to penetrate to reach the heart and beauty of the city with its parks and skyscrapers and peaceful lake.

Our destination, immediately after crossing the busy street, was one particular prairie in No Man's Land which held what we called the swamp — the closest thing we had to a body of water, though the water was actually a spill of muck with the consistency of paint that flowed from the nearby factories, gray, brown, and salmon colored sludge with pools of rusty water floating on top.

Perhaps once or twice a year we ventured this far, just to see the swamp, and always without our parents knowing, though our shoes were wet and clothing tainted upon our return, and we harbored a peculiar smell. "Where were you?" our parents would ask. "Just playing," we replied.

We imagined it a jungle, a wilderness, where one might encounter wild animals and bright colored birds, though little evidence of such life existed but for weeds and foul water. Inevitably a grimness set in. Our games turned more self-absorbing, petulant, seeing who could push whom into the mucky swamp first. Pushing and shoving matches leading to fights,

ending in tears and flight. Someone was always running home hurt and angry. We never stayed long at the swamp. But its very existence, like the factories, remained a compelling attraction. It heightened our everyday fun for no other reason than we were not where we were supposed to be.

As soon as the prairie turned soft under our feet, Davey said, "I know where we are, Hookstra. The swamp. I can smell it. You win, OK? My feet are all wet. Let go of my arm, you jerk. It hurts." Hookstra forced him to sit down in it, then pulled him back up, giving his arm another twist. He was angry that Davey had figured it all out.

"Damn it, Hookstra, that's enough! I'm all wet. Are you happy? My arm is numb. Let's go." I was relieved that it was all over and beginning to get dark. We'd head for home now, racing to get back before the streetlights went on. At least Krachi and I had fooled Davey. He'd be surprised to know we were along.

I thought Hookstra and Davey would be better friends now. At least he didn't cry or try to break away. He'd been a good prisoner, and he didn't even mind that goofy black hat pulled down over his head. He went along with it all once he understood no one was talking, and it was up to him to try and figure out who had captured him and where he was being taken.

Even Krachi thought we had called it quits and began pulling the hat from Davey's head, when suddenly Hookstra punched him in the arm. I expected Hookstra to start laughing now. He would do that sometimes when he lost or had gone too far. He could even reduce your own victory to something

meaningless by laughing at you. He would ease the tension, get out of a losing battle by suddenly turning everything around so you would believe it was all a big joke, exactly the way he had planned, and there were no hard feelings. But Krachi swung back at Hookstra, and neither of them moved. They glared at each other in a standstill, Hookstra still holding onto Davey's arm. Then he motioned with his head for us to follow, and he began walking Davey out of the swamp toward the factories.

Davey began to act silly, which was a side of him we rarely saw. "Hookstra, is this your father's Sunday-go-to-meetin' hat?" he said. "Something he picked up in one of his favorite garbage cans? Hookstra, do you really wear wooden shoes at home?" Then he began raising his knees up high and punching down with his feet in an exaggerated marching step that got us all wet as Hookstra quickly ran him out of the swamp and onto the dry prairie grass. Then all of a sudden Davey began singing: "Go on home, your mother's calling, your father just fell in the garbage can; go on home, your mother's calling, they've come to collect your old man."

"Say, 'I surrender,'" Hookstra whispered into the hat in a rough, foreign sounding voice, grabbing Davey's other arm with a quick twisting motion till he screamed in pain only once, then said nothing, made no other sound again.

We were on the brick streets now, crossing traffic, dodging between parked cars and trucks, walking past fenced factory yards posted with guards at the entrances. The air smelled of burning metal. Freight trains of only a few cars screeched and groaned as they shuttled from one yard to another.

STARS

Hookstra found an empty track and began following it. The silver rails curved into the darkness between two buildings that seemed closed for the night, the loading docks abandoned. Down at the far end stood a single box car. Hookstra led Davey up a small, wooden staircase, and we followed him down the docks. We had never played here before. The possibilities seemed endless. We would have to come back. Krachi and I began jumping on and off the dock between the rails, leaping from one tie to another, balancing ourselves on the rails, our arms stretched to the limits like the wings of dark birds. Then we were springing onto the docks again, catching up to Hookstra and Davey.

It was a single, open boxcar, and Hookstra disappeared into it with Davey. When we got there, he had him in a corner with his face against the wall. But both Krachi and I were so delighted with the thought of an empty boxcar that we began to play and forgot about Davey and Hookstra. I was sure they would soon join us anyway.

We ran from one end of it to the other and through both open doors, paratrooping out the one door onto the ground beside the track. We discovered the small ladder attached and climbed to the top, ran back and forth up there a while, then paratrooped down to the dock. And in all of this we held our voices, though our breath was coming fast.

"Stop!" It was Hookstra's voice from inside the boxcar. As we walked over to him, he grabbed my father's white scarf from around my neck, tied Davey's hands together, then spun him around and around, motioning for us to start running.

Looking over my shoulder I could see Hookstra

struggling to pull the door of the boxcar shut then take off shouting, "Run! Run!" as he passed us. We ran blindly down the dock, onto the railroad bed and out of the yard. Someone behind was blowing a whistle. We split up on the factory streets, the way we often did in our games when something went wrong and there was the danger any one of us could be blamed. I turned a corner and thought I saw both Krachi and Hookstra cross a busy street, safe in their own territory. I could not keep up. The pain in my side from running hurt so much, I had to rest a minute and then walk.

There was no one behind me. I walked past another block of fenced factory yards, thought of going back and walking home with Davey, but was afraid the guards would get me. Besides, it was dark and I wasn't sure I could find the tracks and the boxcar. Factory whistles were blowing. Trucks moving. Trains pulling out of the yards. Machines were pounding the earth so hard I could feel it shudder beneath my feet. I passed a a foundry which seemed all in flames. I passed factory windows that flashed blue and silver and black in steady waves. I passed a fenced war plant with black and yellow Forbidden to Enter signs where a 1941 Plymouth coupe I seemed to recognize was parked against a brick wall beneath a single lightbulb stuck in a cage. It was a car like the one I sometimes saw my mother get out of a few blocks from home on Saturday mornings when I would be out early playing, and occasionally start walking to meet her on her way home from work. I saw a man and a woman kissing in the car and, afraid of being seen, I started running again till I couldn't even feel the pain.

STARS

From the brick street where I stood waiting to cross, clouds of black smoke drifted past occasional patches of stars. In the distance, either moving toward or away from me, I could barely discern the figure of a man and a wagon and a horse.

The streetlights were on in front of my house, as they are now, though the light is so different. I opened the door with my own key and went into the kitchen where my father sat at the table reading the newspaper. "It's late," he said. "Get ready for bed. I'll heat up the soup on the stove."

Nothing more was said, as I recall years later. The war ended. Things changed. We went on to public or parochial high schools. We had our first experiences with girls, fresh, unabiding love that all our lives we would seek to know again with some degree of permanence in other women. We learned to drive our fathers' cars, then bought old ones of our own to customize and paint to suit our taste for speed and color. We kept our hair cropped short like soldiers, or grew it long, swished into D.A.'s with rat-tailed combs, like hoods. Our society was that simple. Some of us went to college; some of us finally went to war. Krachi and Hookstra worked for their fathers, married young, and moved away. Everyone in the neighborhood spoke English. You rarely heard Czech anymore. Mrs. Nactman, a widow, moved to an apartment on the north side of the city. Davey went east to the university, worked in government, remains in the foreign service, assigned somewhere in the Middle East. I have not seen or heard from any of them in almost twenty-five years.

While the neighborhood seemed to diminish in

the absence of us and our childhood games, our earthbound, street-fought fantasies of heroic flight gave way to rockets, space ships, astronauts, galaxies of infinite dimensions we never imagined and might find impossible to play. Only the houses remain, occupied by strangers, forever transient. Children, wherever they may be hiding, do not seem to play here anymore.

On some return visits, before entering my father's house again, I take to the brightly lit street at night, aware I am the only one walking the neighborhood in this hour. I stand on the corner where the war memorial once stood, remembering how the concrete star cracked in time and weeds grew through, how the white picket fence and flagpole lost their paint, how one time after the war a new garbage truck came from the city and hauled everything away. Walking toward the factories, I realize the swamp is buried beneath a huge shopping center, no prairie remains, and the factories were never as far away as I imagined. They are there still — fenced yards, pounding machinery, railroads cars — all of it under the same orange glow as the neighborhood streets, but even more radiant, more intense, as the light finds the smoke-filled atmosphere impenetrable, and the neighborhood, the factories, the city are indistinguishable under the same burning sky.

My mother said she could read the writing on the wall, soon after the war. In the last few years of her life, she felt the place was changing for the worst, was afraid to go out at night, wanted to move, and tried to get my father to find another house somewhere in a quiet suburb. "But this is home," he said. He still believes things remain pretty much the same. He

STARS

leaves the house but once a day, at noon, when things seem safest. He shops and brings home junk from the alley. "If you leave people alone," he says, "they'll leave you alone." Since Krachi's died, their house next door has been sold five different times. The new people have lived there for two years, but he hasn't met them yet. "Hillbillies," he says, who turn their music up so loud day and night he'd like to tell them something.

Though my old key still fits the front door, I cannot open it anymore. I must use a code now, he's devised, tapping the window glass with the key six times, while he checks through the blinds to see who's there before he unlocks the door from the inside.

"It's you," he says. "Just like daylight out there, ain't it? You can see everything, only too much of it gets in the house at night."

He wears a large pair of women's sunglasses he's found in the alley and fixed, bending a straight pin through the broken hinge. "These help," he says. The orange glow of the high sodium lights in every street and alley creates a false feeling of night, a dead light in which no one sleeps well anymore.

"They still haven't put that stone on your mother's grave," he says. "As long as I can find it, what's the difference?" We sit in the parlor. Light streams in through the venetian blinds and falls on him in horizontal patterns that rise and fall in the movement of the leafy branches of the tree outside the window.

"So take off your hat and coat and stay awhile," he says. I wear some of his old clothes which he has given me because he has more clothes than he can

ever wear for as long as he lives, he tells me. I dangle his old fedora by the brim, between my legs, the way us used to sit.

"So where you been now?" he asks. "What's next? I'm used to this, alone. It's all the same."

That night as a child when I returned home late from the factories, turned off the light in my room, and climbed into bed, I remember looking up and feeling the roof of the house had been blown off. My ceiling was covered with paper stars that glowed in the dark. I felt dizzy in the way as children we would whirl and whirl ourselves around in the backyard on summer nights, our eyes fixed to the deep heavens, mouths agape, arms outstretched, till we lost our balance, falling finally, we were certain, into the stars.

The wooden window blinds rattled halfway up with a crack, as my mother yanked the cord the next morning, thrust the window up, filling the room with sunlight and cool air. "How did you like your surprise?" she asked. "Did you see the stars last night? Weren't they beautiful? Here, Davey returned your scarf while you were sleeping. You better not let your father see it."

I lay there a long time, the scarf around my neck, pulling and holding on tightly to the fringes in my hands, staring at the white ceiling in search of stars scattered about the daylight of the room.

In the dead of night in my father's house, we each retire to our old bedrooms, leaving the doors ajar. "Jesus," I hear him sigh from his bed.

I lay in the emptiness of my room, putting everything back in place, struggling to find the words ... *I believe ... in all things ... invisible ...*

PS
3552
.L42
G48
1986